The Christmas Cowboy Competition

Horseshoe Home Ranch

LIZ ISAACSON

ISBN-13: 978-1-63876-244-7

"Fear thou not; for I am with thee: be not dismayed;
for I am thy God: I will strengthen thee; yea, I will
help thee; yea, I will uphold thee with the right hand
of my righteousness."

— ISAIAH 41:10

CHAPTER 1

Archer Bailey stepped out into the tiny backyard of his townhome and inhaled. Ah, yes. The crisp scent of freshly mowed grass mingled with the underlying scent of mountain water and a slightly chlorinated whiff from the pool a few hundred yards away.

Today was the day. Today, he was going to land the job that would start his career. Today was the day his life would change.

He lifted his hand to his black cowboy hat, the hint of fall already in the valley though Labor Day still lingered a week away. Sometimes Montana saw snow in September, and Archer loved it. Loved everything about Gold Valley, and horses, and hopefully, Horseshoe Home Ranch, where he had an interview in three short hours.

Then his father could stop riding him for quitting college. For giving up a scholarship Archer had earned by the skin of his teeth and pure luck. For coming home without a job or a direction he wanted to go in.

His little buckskin-colored dog sniffed around his feet as the sliding glass door just across the fence opened. Carrot Cake immediately started barking, easing when the gorgeous blonde removed her hat and crouched, extending the tips of her fingers through the slats in the fence to give Carrot a scrap of cheese.

"You know he's on a diet," Archer said, trying not to rake his gaze up and down Emersyn Ender's body. They'd lived next door to each other for two years. Shared a wall, a fence, and his dog for twenty-four long months.

At first, Archer had thought they could make a go of a relationship. But Emery radiated a coldness he'd never experienced, not even in the depths of a Montana January. She held everything close to the vest, rarely said more than five words to him, and kept mostly to herself.

"He looks like he's lost some weight."

"Hmph." Archer sipped his coffee, sure Carrot Cake had only lost a few ounces and only because of the grooming Archer had done on him late last week.

"How's the job hunt going?" She tucked her hands into the back pockets of her shorts and looked beyond him, over the waist-high fence that separated their private yards from the common areas of the complex. She always did this sort of looking past him thing, like he was some foul ogre she couldn't bear to look directly at.

He shifted his feet self-consciously, wanting to keep his

job interview a secret. After all, Emery had stolen his last opportunity right out from under him.

That's not fair, he thought immediately, but the familiar disappointment and his old friend bitterness pressed against the back of his tongue anyway.

"I have an interview today," he said, unsure of when his brain had told his vocal chords to speak.

Emery focused on him, her bright blue eyes startling and absolutely beautiful. Archer took another gulp of coffee. "That's great, Archie."

So she had a nickname for him. He hated it. Didn't mean they were friends.

"Where?" she asked.

"Oh, up at the ranch." Four ranches surrounded Gold Valley, and he kept it vague on purpose. "How are things at Silver Creek?"

They'd both gone out for the same job at the teen rehabilitation center last spring. In the end, the director there decided he wanted a female equestrian trainer where he'd always, always had a male. She'd gotten the job. Archer had slunk home like a pup with its tail between his legs. He waited for her to take her garbage can out on Wednesdays so he didn't run into her. Then he brought both cans in at night to avoid her further. The lengths he'd gone to in order to save face had astounded even him.

Emery sighed, a long drawn-out hiss that raised an alarm in Archer's system. "It's fine. But my twelve-week program ends on Friday. Then I'm out of a job."

"Oh." Archer didn't know what else to say. His first inclination was to ask if her job would be available, but he didn't want to seem overeager or rude or unsympathetic. Truth was, he felt a kindred soul in Emery as she'd bounced from as many jobs as he had over the years. She didn't seem to have a parent rubbing her nose in it though.

"Good luck with your interview." Emery flashed him a smile that, if she'd allow it to reach her eyes and light up her whole face, would be a sight to behold. She tucked her hair behind her ear and went back inside her house, much to Carrot Cake's disconcertion.

"Oh, quiet down, you." Archer toed the whiny dog back into his own townhouse and shut out the world. Shut out Emery. Shut out everything. He needed to find his center if today was really going to be the day that started his life.

He dropped to a sitting position in the living room and crossed his legs. With his eyes closed, he prayed in a whisper, "Please help me say all the right things during the interview."

Please, please, please pretty much dominated the rest of his meditation session. By the time he left to get up to Horseshoe Home Ranch, Archer wasn't sure if any of his prayers or the minutes he spent meditating actually did anything but waste time.

———

Emery didn't waste a single moment after she left Archer standing in his backyard. He hadn't told her where the job was—purposefully, she knew—but she had a laptop and their community provided fantastic fiber Internet service as part of the HOA fees.

It only took her a single search and a quick scan of one job board to find the listing for a cowhand at Horseshoe Home Ranch. She worried the inside of her cheek with her teeth as she read the description. She'd grown up on a small farm in Wyoming until age twelve; she'd ridden horses since the age of five, and had begun training them when her father left them all behind. But she'd seen him tag cows, and fix fences, and move sprinkler pipes. How hard could it be?

And bonus, she knew Jace and Belle Lovell from church. Well, "knew" was probably a huge stretch, but at this point, Emery had to play every advantage she had. She needed a job, one that paid well enough to keep her in this townhome and allowed her to keep sending money to her sister in Spokane.

The twinges of guilt strumming through her body were easily covered by the desperate need to keep Glenna going. Her sister worked at a big box store, paid her own rent, and scraped by with cheap groceries bought with her employee discount. Emery paid all the utilities. The Adult Services group in Spokane provided her transportation, so that was a relief.

She jotted down the number for the ranch, stuffing the last moments of regret to the soles of her feet. It was a job. Heaven knew Archer wasn't the only candidate for it, and just because Emery wanted to throw her hat into the ring didn't mean he didn't have a good chance.

"Better than you," she mumbled to herself as she carefully punched in the numbers. The line rang and her stomach did flips. One, two, three. Finally a woman said, "Hello?"

"Yes, hello, I'm calling about the cowhand job. Is it still available?"

"Uh, let's see." Scratching came through the line, something like the shuffling of papers. "Yes, today's the last morning of interviews. Looks like we're booked, though. Let me see…." More scuffling and then a loud *bang!* hurt Emery's ears.

"Oh my stars." The woman's tinny voice sounded light years away. "I'm so sorry," she said normally now. "I dropped the phone. Can I give you a call back in a few minutes? I'll go talk to Jace and see if he can do one more interview, all right?"

"Sure, yeah, all right." Though she didn't want to end the call without a scheduled appointment—especially if today was the last day Jace was doing interviews—Emery didn't really see what other choice she had. She gave the woman her name and phone number and hung up.

She needed to be over at Silver Creek by two o'clock, but the woman had said "morning of interviews" so hopefully Emery could do both.

A high-pitched whirring sound came from the townhouse to her left—Archer's place. She'd never asked him what he did every morning to make that sound, but it lasted less than a minute, and Emery had assumed it was a high-end blender. *Probably a smoothie junkie,* she thought, adding an eyeroll to her mental musings.

Emery never ate breakfast and rarely consumed more than fruits, nuts, and vitamin water anyway. Her stomach didn't seem to play nicely with much more. She paced from her kitchen to her front door, which took about ten steps. Turn. Pace back.

She had more productive things to do around the house, like fold laundry and clean bathrooms, but she couldn't seem to make her mind settle on anything but the job at Horseshoe Home.

Eventually, she pulled out the disinfectant wipes and swept them over countertops, light switches, and walls, waiting for her phone to ring. She did all the dishes and had just moved into the half-bath to get the toilet sparkling when her device finally chirped.

She scrambled for it and breathlessly answered the unknown number. "Emery?" the woman asked. "It's Belle from Horseshoe Home. Jace says he's happy to have you come up this morning. Does eleven o'clock work for you?"

"Yes, absolutely, sure." Emery checked herself and took a big breath. "I'll be there."

"Great." Belle wore a smile in her voice. "The interview will be in his office, which is in the administration lodge. It's the second biggest house up here, on the right-hand side of the road."

"Sounds good." Emery hung up and pressed her eyes closed. Now she just needed to get this job so she could continue to help her sister maintain her lifestyle.

A few hours later, Emery seated herself in the run-down Jeep she used for a vehicle. The engine had almost two-hundred-fifty thousand miles on it, but it was still trucking along. Emery had named the Jeep Jenny at the first hundred thousand miles, and she prayed every morning and every night that her car would be spared any wear and tear, that it would keep running, and so far God had granted her that minor miracle.

She exited the community where she lived and turned right. The canyon and the glorious horseshoe shaped falls bloomed before her very eyes, and a quick rush of gratitude reminded her of how lucky she was to live in such a beautiful place.

The ranch only sat twenty minutes from her front door, and she arrived earlier than she'd anticipated. Butterflies the size of dinner plates crashed into her abdominal lining, and she thought sure she'd need to throw up before entering the appointed building.

With one final cramp and a deep breath, Emery left Jenny's safety and mounted the front steps. Through the doors, she came to a desk with a weathered cowboy sitting behind it.

"Mornin', ma'm," he said. "You here for the interviews?"

"Yes, sir."

"Chair right there." He pointed with the pen he held in his right hand toward an empty row of white folding chairs. At least she didn't have to see any of the other applicants. Her own cowgirl boots clicked against the tile as she made her way to the chairs and sat.

Eleven o'clock came and went. A few cowboys worked in the open area filled with desks. Laughter came from a doorway in the back that had bright fluorescent lights spilling from it. The scent of marinara and meat came from that direction too, and Emery's stomach grumbled. A hallway sat across from the kitchen and went left into areas she couldn't see.

Impatience gnawed at her thoughts, making her right toe tap, tap, tap against the tile. She had no idea how long this interview would take, and she still needed to grab lunch and get all the way across town to Silver Creek by two.

Finally, finally, after sitting there for a half an hour—and twenty of those minutes were past her appointed interview time—a pair of men appeared in the hallway. They paused, and Emery's focus razored in on them.

One—the slightly taller man—was Jace Lovell, owner. The other—with his signature black cowboy hat—was Archer Bailey, rival and neighbor.

Panic poured through Emery in waves. He would see her. There was no way he *wouldn't* see her. She needed to move now.

Now!

But her body remained as limp and lifeless as a sack of potatoes. Everything slowed around her except her pulse, which only seemed to be accelerating. Faster and faster while everything else blurred behind a layer of wax paper.

Jace smiled. The two of them shook hands. Archer turned toward her. He stepped, and stepped, Jace right behind him.

Why did it take so long for him to make it to the front of

the room? Why was Emery's chest so tight? Why did her fingers ache and pulse with their own heartbeat?

"Emery?" The level of surprise in Archer's voice shocked Emery out of the weird warpy thing that had just happened. "What are you doing here?"

She leapt to her feet, every cell in her body buzzing like someone had hooked her to a live wire and turned the electricity up high.

"She's my last interview," Jace said, joining them and extending his hand for Emery to shake. "C'mon back, Emery. Good to see you again, Archer." He turned and walked away, but Emery couldn't move.

Archer glared at her with more menace than she knew he possessed. He'd always been nice to her, probably nicer than he should've been given how little attention she'd given him over the years. He brought her garbage can in when it snowed heavily, and he'd fixed her fence when the gate slammed into it.

He could've said all kinds of things in this situation. Breathed threats at her. Delved into a long lecture about his disgust for her. All of it was plain to see right there in his deep, dark eyes. Eyes that had always sucked at Emery's resolve, always beckoned that if she just dove in, she'd like what happened after that.

He said nothing. Just marched past her and out the door.

CHAPTER 2

Fury boiled in Archer's gut, and he did not like it. No, he did not like it, not one little bit. Somehow he managed to navigate his toy-sized truck down the canyon without smashing into a cement barrier or going off the road and hitting a tree. A small miracle, really, given the level of annoyance altering his vision.

By the time he pulled into his driveway, the smell of hot rubber and the sharp metallic scent of his engine filled the cab. He really couldn't push his truck like that; it was barely hanging on to the last days of its life. And Archer had no way to pay to replace it or repair it. He would not be asking his father, who had talent under the hood of a vehicle.

Still, he practically gunned the engine once the garage door lifted, nearly crashed right into the deep freezer he had against the back wall, which held a box of corndogs and several cartons of pistachio ice cream.

He snatched the corndogs on his way inside and threw

them on the counter, startling Carrot Cake. The little dog whined, and Archer softened. "Sorry, bud. But you would not believe that woman." He spun to turn on the oven, nearly knocking over the high-powered blender that he used every morning for his protein shakes.

"I can't believe her. I—just—can't—believe—" He stopped talking, his frustration so foul he couldn't even form coherent words. He put three corndogs on a baking tray and slammed it into the still-warming-up oven. He made loud *cracks!* and *bangs!* as he got out the ketchup and mayo and mixed up a dipping sauce for his meager lunch.

His mother would caution him to put something green on the plate. "Or some grapes, Arch. *Something* from the plant family." Her voice rebounded through his head. At least she only lectured him about his dietary choices. His father lectured him about *all* of his choices, and Archer pulled an apple from the fridge and chomped into it while he waited for the rest of his food to cook.

The full twenty minutes for the corndogs to bake passed before Archer felt his fury fade. He didn't want to be home when Emery returned, so he packed everything onto a plate and went back out to his truck. He managed to leave his house and get down the street without seeing her. Thankfully. He couldn't predict what he'd do next time he came face-to-face with her.

Moments later, he pulled into the parking lot at the waterfalls and got out. With school starting last week, there were noticeably less families here, and he found a table easily. Desperation coated his tongue along with the grease from the corndogs. What would he do if he lost another job to Emery Ender?

His mind imploded at the very thought of it. He'd have to move. And not just across town. But out of state.

She'd never rubbed in the fact that she'd been hired at Silver Creek over him, but Archer's pride wouldn't allow him to live next door to her if she got this job and he didn't. No way. Couldn't happen.

He needed this job, and not only because it was a job that would pay the bills. He needed it to start his career. He needed it to show his father he wasn't going to bounce from temp job to temp job for the next twenty years. He needed it to boost his own confidence, which seemed to have fallen in the gutter last Christmas and made a permanent home there.

The interview had gone great. Archer had practically floated toward the front of the administration lodge—until his gaze had landed on Emery. Everything inside him had revved up and then shut down, almost within the same breath. He'd learned from his father that sometimes saying nothing was more hurtful than yelling, so he'd strode out without a backward glance.

"Better get a back-up plan, Arch," he told himself. He pulled out his phone and navigated to the online job boards for Gold Valley. He'd have better luck securing a more long-term job in a bigger city, but he loved the town where he'd grown up. His parents still lived in the four-bedroom blue house in Monkeytown, and both of his brothers had left for their careers, leaving him with the responsibility of looking after the house and his parents as everything aged.

Archer didn't mind. He didn't have a fancy computer science degree like Charlie; didn't design the biggest video games on the market while sipping skinny mocha lattes and wearing hippie sandals around Bellevue, Washington. Archer also didn't have a highfalutin engineering degree like Xan, who lived in Huntsville, Alabama and worked for NASA.

Seriously, *NASA?* How was Archer supposed to compete with that?

But compete his father expected. So when Archer had dropped out of college and moved into a townhome he could barely make the payment on, his father's disappointment carried on the wind from his house across town.

Archer had been looking for something he could do as a career and not have a degree for. He loved hiking, being outside with the fresh air and the scent of pines. He loved horses, and had thought for a couple of weeks there that he could make a career out of working with wayward boys and horses.

That hadn't worked out, but Archer had learned that he was supposed to be a cowboy. He just needed a ranch that was hiring. He'd checked the job boards every day for seventy-three days before a job came up at Horseshoe Home.

He got to his feet and tossed his trash in the nearby can. And that blasted Emery Ender had honed in on his job, had dared to call and get an interview that very morning. He shook his head, wanting to be angry, but his emotions had been spent.

Still unwilling to go home until he knew Emery would be at work, he went to McCall's, the gas station that used to mark the edge of town, back before all the new housing developments closer to the falls and the mouth of the canyon had been built.

"Afternoon, Arch," Myron said from his perch on the counter-high stool just inside the convenience store. He sat in the window and watched all the comings and goings of Gold Valley. Archer had never seen the man wear anything but jean overalls with either a blue, a yellow, or a white shirt underneath. And Myron always chewed a piece of peppermint gum. "Keeps my breath minty," he'd told Archer when he'd asked about it.

"Afternoon." Archer went over to the cooler and pulled out a sports drink. He paid and then sagged his weight against the counter, the indentation there from the countless people who'd come to the gas station for refills and refreshment and gotten it in more ways than one.

"What's eatin' you?"

"Nothing." Archer took a swig from his bottle.

"Right." Myron cocked one eyebrow at him, and Archer whipped off his hat to mimic the action.

Myron ducked his left and seemed to get his right all the way to his hairline. Archer smiled as he repeated the action. He wiggled one up and down while the other stayed still. Myron filled the convenience store with laughter and waved one hand. "You win."

"I always do." He sobered when he realized how untrue the words really were. "Can I ask you a question?"

"Sure."

"You've owned this station and store for a while, right?"

"Forty-seven years. My daddy owned it before that."

Archer actually envied that kind of stability. The idea that Myron knew what his life would be and had embraced it. "Exactly."

"Exactly what?"

"I applied for a job today," Archer said, not really sure where he was going with the conversation. "I really want it."

Myron simply waited, his eyes watching the gas pumps and his lips smacking as he chewed, chewed, chewed that gum.

"So if you had a job you really wanted, what would you do to get it?" Archer asked.

Myron took a long time to lift one of his beefy shoulders, today's yellow shirt bunching where his arm met his body. He wore a dark gray cowboy hat—the same one Archer had seen dozens of times before.

"Yeah, I don't know either," Archer said. He glanced around the old store, appreciating the vintage signs, the way the coolers kept on humming, the scent of nacho cheese and warming hot dogs on rollers.

"Oh, I know," Myron said just as the bell on the door chimed and a mother entered with her two preschool-age children.

Archer glanced at them but focused quickly back on Myron when he said, "I'd fight for it. Do everything I could to get it." He shrugged his other shoulder this time. "I mean, if it was what I wanted."

Nodding, Archer stepped out of the way so the woman could buy her gas and her children's suckers.

He couldn't make Jace give him the job. Archer would get a phone call with a decision. How was he supposed to fight that?

———

Emery was not expecting to see anyone sitting on her front porch when her headlights cut a swath of light across the front lawn she shared with Archer. She pulled all the way into her garage, her heart tip-tapping out an irregular beat.

She kept Jenny running and the doors locked while she waited for the garage door to come down. Only then did she dare turn off the car and go into her house. Seconds later, someone knocked.

A man, judging by the heavy fistfalls.

Emery knew who it was. And she knew Archer wouldn't go away. She'd really hoped to avoid this confrontation. She'd been relieved when she'd returned home from her interview to find his place silent, dormant. And at nine-thirty-five PM, after her shift at Silver Creek, she honestly hadn't expected he'd want to do this tonight.

"C'mon, Emery," he called through the door. "I know you're in there."

She deposited her purse and keys on the kitchen counter

and went to the door, yanking it open right when he was about to beat on it again.

He lowered his fist and then stuck it in his pocket. He wore jeans that hugged his thighs in all the right ways, that delicious cowboy hat, and a shirt the color of apricots. She wanted to laugh at him about the shirt, but he made the soft peachy color look sexy, and all she could do was lick her lips and wait for him to chew her out.

She deserved it. She shouldn't have looked up his job and applied for it. Regret had been lancing through her all afternoon, especially when Dr. Richards had given a lesson on integrity to all the girls right before their riding lesson. Apparently, he'd been having a problem with theft at Silver Creek, and he wanted the girls to know that integrity was about more than just being honest.

Before Archer could say anything, Emery said, "I'm sorry, Archie. I shouldn't have gone up there this morning."

He blinked at her, his strong jaw muscle twitching as his teeth ground together. She sighed and stepped back, a clear invitation for him to enter her house. He didn't, and she was glad he didn't. She'd never invited him inside before, and she didn't know why she'd thought now would be a good idea.

"I can't even do that job," she said. "Jace asked me about lifting a hay bale, and wrestling with a full-grown cow to give medication." She gave a mirthless laugh to go with this miserable day. "And there's no way I can set a fence post by myself. He said cowhands often do that kind of stuff." Sure, she had some experience from her childhood, but she simply wasn't as strong as a man.

Archer just stood there, and she wondered how long he'd been waiting on her porch, and why he wouldn't say something.

She finally asked, "What do you want?"

"Why do you need this job so badly?" he asked.

"I have bills to pay." She folded her arms across her chest, as if that would somehow keep the truth inside.

He shook his head slowly, everything about him a shadow from his raven hair, those dark diamond eyes, and his black cowboy hat. "There has to be more than that going on here."

"Why's that?" She cleared her throat when her voice strayed into an upper octave.

"You just admitted that you've applied for a job you can't do. Why don't you go, oh, I don't know. Waitress or work at the elementary school or be a checker at the grocery store?"

She settled her weight onto her back foot, the fight in her rearing to the front of her skull. "Oh, and leave the real work to the men, is that it?"

"No."

"You do realize there are male waiters, right? And teachers too, shockingly."

"Of course. I just meant—"

"I know what you meant."

"No, you don't," he argued. "I meant that—just—why apply for a job you can't do when there are tons you can?"

The dull ache behind her eyes she'd been fighting for

hours started to throb. She needed to eat and take some painkiller and get to bed. She couldn't stand here in her doorway for much longer, breathing in the woodsy quality of Archer's skin or the fresh waterfall scent of his clothes.

"I'm sorry," she said again. "I'll call up to the ranch in the morning and tell Belle I can't do it, that they shouldn't consider me."

"They?" Archer asked.

"Yeah, Belle came into my interview too." She frowned and leaned forward to peer at him. He seemed genuinely confused. "She wasn't at yours?"

"No." He clipped out the word like a bullet, and she had the distinct feeling he really disliked her. *That's good,* she told herself even though she wanted the opposite. So maybe she'd dreamt of him banging on her door in the dead of night—but for an entirely different reason.

She shook her head to clear it. Having fantasies about her sexy next-door neighbor wouldn't make sure Glenna's heat stayed on this winter.

"She was already in Jace's office when I got back there," she said. "I assumed she'd helped him with all the interviews."

Archer glared at her. He must practice for an hour every morning with how he'd perfected the narrow squint of his eyes and the extreme distaste pouring from every pore of his skin.

"Whatever," he finally said. "I just wanted you to know that I think you did a lousy thing today."

Her heart flopped like a fish on dry land. "I know I did, Archie. I'm sorry."

"Sometimes sorry—" He cut off as his phone sounded in tandem with hers. Her simple, factory-chosen chime didn't mesh with his custom *twill-a-will!* that echoed through the night sky after it finally finished.

He glanced at his phone; she at hers. Anything for a distraction.

This is Jace Lovell. Can you come for a second interview tomorrow at nine o'clock?

Her pulse catapulted around various points of her body, finally landing back in its rightful place in her chest. A smile pulled at the corners of her mouth, and she glanced up at Archer, who wore a grin so delightful she wondered what it felt like to be that happy.

"I have a second interview tomorrow," he said.

"Me too." She twisted her phone so he could see the message from Jace.

His smile vanished, replaced by a scowl and then a frown of confusion. "Mine's at nine too. That makes no sense."

"Maybe it's a group interview?" she guessed.

He wandered around the partition separating their front doors, his attention on his phone. He went inside without saying anything, almost like he'd forgotten Emery even stood there. With the final click of his door, she pushed hers closed too, her headache now pounding through her whole body.

She could only hope and pray he'd forgive her, just like she'd been hoping and praying he'd finally wake up and *see* her standing right where she'd always been—next door.

$\mathcal{E}$mery waited until she'd be late to leave the house, and still Archer hadn't left his. With a jolt of understanding, she realized he was probably waiting for her to leave first. So she hit her garage door opener and situated herself behind the wheel of Jenny. Movement in her rearview mirror showed Archer and his gray truck backing out, confirming her theory.

Hundreds of tiny feet clawed through her stomach. She shouldn't even be going up to the ranch. If she didn't show up, she wouldn't be considered for the job. Easy. Done. Her mistake in encroaching on Archer's job would be over. Forgiven.

And yet, she couldn't help herself from going. It was a job. And in four short days, she'd need a new one.

So she got herself and Jenny up the canyon and into a parking spot on the packed dirt road housing the ranch's main buildings. There seemed to be a lot more vehicles here than yesterday, and her anxiety skyrocketed. How big was this group interview going to be anyway?

Noise assaulted her as soon as she stepped into the administration lodge. So did the scent of cinnamon and frosting, with a hint of something fruity. As soon as she spotted a cowboy with a clear plastic cup of orange juice, the smell of citrus hit her square in the face.

There seemed to be some sort of continental breakfast set up on a long table just outside the kitchen. No one sat at the reception desk, and Emery had no idea where to go or what to do.

A man caught her eye and waved for her to come on back. Somehow she got her feet moving in the right direction, and a tall cowboy with a jovial smile told her to get some breakfast and they'd be meeting in the kitchen in a few minutes.

Emery took a cinnamon roll—which looked homemade —and a cup of orange juice. She wondered who on earth even made cinnamon rolls from scratch anymore as she sipped her juice in the pretense of eating.

"Let's go," a man bellowed, and every cowboy in the building snapped to attention, flowing into the kitchen like God himself had spoken.

And He sort of had, because Jace Lovell stood at the front of the room, his sharp eyes missing nothing and no one.

"Quiet down, quiet down." Jace picked up a piece of paper from the table beside him. "I need my new recruits up here, front and center."

In that moment, Emery was extremely glad she had chosen to forego eating the cinnamon roll. She certainly couldn't be known as the woman who hurled because she had to stand in front of a room of men.

As she joined four other men—one of which was Archer—she in fact realized she was the only woman in the room. Her legs trembled but she couldn't lock them for fear of fainting.

"So we've got Bentley, Clyde, Lars, Archer, and Emersyn." Jace glanced at each of them in turn when he said their names. He turned back toward the cowboys who already had jobs. "They're going to be your competition this fall."

A whoop rose into the air, something Emery didn't understand. She glanced down the row of men she stood beside, and they didn't seem to know either.

"I need to hire one of these fine people," Jace said, pacing in front of them. "And we've gotten lazy around the ranch. So, starting today, everyone gets their chores from the board. You'll work with a different partner every day, and for the first week, we'll be training. Myself, Tom, and Ty will come around and check work and award stars." He nodded as two men—Tom and Ty, assumedly—came up to the front of the room. Jace then held up a sheet of gold stars, which made some of the men practically salivate.

Emery felt so far out of her league. No way she was winning a star over any of these cowboys. Some of them looked like they ate women her size for breakfast.

"Belle made us a nice sticker chart and everything." One of the important men who would decide everything pulled a sheet off the wall to reveal a very professional-looking chart, a column for every cowhand on the ranch.

"I'm competing this year too," Jace said, and the twittering in the crowd quieted.

"You are?" one of the cowboys asked.

Jace turned back to his staff. "It's been a while since I've been out there, doing what you guys do. Sometimes a man forgets, and I don't want to be the boss who doesn't know what his cowboys have to put up with." He shrugged, but Emery could tell this was a big deal to him.

"So let this year's annual contest begin!"

———

Archer couldn't believe his good fortune. No, he didn't have a steady job. But as he filled out his tax paperwork and handed over his driver's license to Belle so she could make a copy, his chest filled with hope.

He was going to work at Horseshoe Home for the next four months. Honest, paid work. The contest ran through Christmas, at which time the temporary cowhand with the most stars would be hired.

Hired.

Archer had never wanted something so badly.

He caught Emery with her head bent close to Jace's. They had a conversation that didn't look like it ended well for her, but she filled out all the papers too. His stomach soured every time he caught a whiff of her raspberry and brown sugar scent, wondering where it came from. Her shampoo or her perfume? A body wash maybe? Or maybe she stirred some sort of fancy-schmancy brown sugar into her morning coffee.

No matter what, Emery took up way too much mental space inside Archer's mind. He really needed to change that if he was going to win this contest, win this job, win this career.

He got paired with a man named Elliott who looked to be about five or six years older than Archer's twenty-five. While they waited for Jace and Ty to fill out the assignment boards, Archer learned that Elliott lived right here on the ranch—that all the cowboys did.

The idea of giving up his townhome—and the expense of it—only sent more excitement through Archer. "You married?" he asked Elliott, shooting a glance at Emery. Which was just plain stupid, as he was still pretty angry with her for even being here.

"No," Elliott said. "But some of the boys are." He glanced toward the hall when someone appeared, but it wasn't Jace. "You?"

"No," Archer said.

"You ever worked a ranch before?"

Archer had a hard time swallowing, but he said "No," anyway.

"It's not hard," Elliott said. "Well, there are a lot of hard things about it, but I think you'll do just fine."

Jace and Ty appeared then, and the tension in the room skyrocketed. "We work until the job's done," Jace said. "Then we ask for another task. There's always something to do in the fall on a ranch this size. So if you finish your chore, radio in and one of us will come check it. Then we'll give you somethin' else."

He stepped away from the board and the crowd of cowboys swarmed. Archer wanted to press forward and find his name, but he hung back, unsure of himself or even where to go. He lost track of Elliott for several seconds, and then found him wearing a huge smile as he waved Archer toward the door.

Thankful to leave the mob behind, Archer hurried after his partner. "What did we get?"

"Bullpen fence check," Elliott said, pushing out of the administration lodge. "The bullpen is back behind the barns, way out at the end of the lane. We check the fences, make sure the bulls seem healthy and happy, and give them fresh food and water. It's an hour-long job, tops."

"And that's good?"

"Sure," Elliott practically skipped down the steps. "It's an easy job, number one. We'll probably both get stars. And then we'll get another job quick. Chance for another star."

Archer smiled, finally understanding. "Do you guys do this every year?"

"I wish." Elliott strode down a dirt road in front of a row of well-kept cowboy cabins. Archer wanted to live in one so badly, his throat tightened. "Jace gets this idea in his head about every three or four years. He needs new people, but he doesn't want to take forever to train them. He thinks those of us that have been here a while are gettin' lazy. And like he said, he likes to get out on the ranch every now and then and remind himself why he's a cowboy."

Elliott could walk fast, and Archer had a hard time keeping up. His breathing turned ragged, and he thought maybe he should invest in a pair of running shoes instead of these slippery cowboy boots.

"He changes it up," Elliott continued, a bit winded himself. "Last time, it was a point system. I like the idea of stars." He pointed way down the road. "That's Tom's cabin. He's Jace's brother. The bull pen is a few hundred yards beyond that."

Archer had never been as close to a bull as he got only a few minutes later. Nearly eye-to-eye, and a thrill ran from the top of his head to the soles of his feet. He watched Elliott, asked questions, did his best.

And sure enough, only an hour later, both he and Elliott had earned a star from the foreman, Ty, and were on their way back to the administration lodge to get another assignment.

"Great job." Elliott held up his hand for Archer to high five, which he did. Archer had just earned more than a gold star. He'd gotten a measure of pride back that he'd lost. And maybe he'd just made a friend too.

CHAPTER 4

*A*rcher didn't see Emery for the rest of the day. He could barely figure out where on the ranch he was, as he and Elliott went from task to task like Tasmanian devils. All the cowboys worked at the same feverish pace they did, and Archer wondered how long they could feasibly keep this up.

Jace finally rang a huge bell from the front porch of his homestead about six o'clock. Archer glanced around for Emery, but she wasn't there. Had she quit? For some reason, that made a balloon of hope inflate beneath his heart.

He immediately regretted the feeling, his emotions warring with themselves. But they couldn't both have this job. Just because he found her attractive and alluring didn't mean he was going to let her beat him again. No, he was going to do what Myron had said and fight for this job.

"Great work today, boys," Jace called. "Belle's got dinner on in the house." He held up his hand as the crowd started to swell forward. "Some of us are new, and some of us forget that this is my wife's home. Let's treat it the way we'd treat our own homes and wives, all right?"

He turned and opened the door, cowboys already joining him on the porch. Archer followed, his stomach growling like a grizzly bear. Everything about Horseshoe Home Ranch was better than he'd imagined.

His muscles cramped as he climbed the stairs, and he anticipated having a very painful night ahead of him, with soreness in his arms and abs in the morning. But he didn't care. He'd put in a good day's work. Work he liked. Work he could see himself doing for years to come.

And he'd never felt that way about anything before.

The scene inside the house felt familial, and Archer soaked up the warmth of it, the camaraderie, the easy ribbing of one cowboy to another. Elliott stayed by him, and Archer noticed all the new recruits had what looked to be the most veteran cowboys assigned to them.

"How long have you worked here?" Archer asked as he picked up a paper plate and put a square of cornbread on it.

Elliott took three pieces of cornbread and a huge dollop of "the best raspberry butter you'll ever eat. Miss Belle grows the berries herself." He grinned at Archer. "And I've been here about twelve years now."

"Wow." Archer's curiosity bubbled inside him. "So this is something you can do as a career, right?"

"Sure." Elliott bypassed the green salad and went for the mustardy potato salad instead. "Look at Jace and Tom and

Ty. They're in this for their whole lives. Nelson—the general controller—he's been here for thirty-one years."

Archer glanced around, finding some younger men and some older men. Some right in the middle. Something soft and feathery tickled his mind, almost like a whisper saying, *This is what your life could be like, Archer. This right here.*

He smiled and put a few pieces of lettuce and tomato on his plate to make his mother proud.

The sun had already sunk behind the mountains by the time he got home. His automatic light came on with the movement of his truck down the driveway. He eased himself from the vehicle and groaned as he went inside. Though it had been one of the best days of his life, it had also been one of the most tiring.

Everything hurt, from his head to his pinched left pinky toe. He swallowed four ibuprofen pills with a bottle of water and kicked off his boots. He shed his clothes completely and collapsed into bed, only home for five minutes before he was fast asleep.

Pounding woke him. He lifted his cheek from the bedspread where he'd fallen, trying to place it. Front door? One of his shared walls?

It didn't come again, and he laid his head back down. His phone went off in the next moment, and he sat up to check it. First he needed to find it, and as it continued going off, he located it easily in the back pocket of his fallen jeans.

How many stars did you earn?

Emery.

Archer grinned as he typed *3 today.*

I had to go back to work, she'd messaged, followed by, *Can I get a ride with you in the morning? And maybe take your truck down to Silver Creek? Jenny broke down tonight.*

Concern wove through him. Though he and Emery weren't the closest of friends, he borrowed coffee from her on occasion, and they'd always helped each other when they had car problems.

Archer would rather call than text, but it was late, and he knew Emery hated talking on the phone. So he gave his thumbs an additional workout and told her he'd be happy to give her a ride up to the ranch. He asked what was wrong with Jenny, and said he could get someone to give him a ride home so she could take his truck to her other job.

I can come get you during my dinner break, she messaged.

The thought of two twenty-minute car rides, alone with Emery, accelerated Archer's pulse in a way it hadn't been accelerated in a while. He wasn't sure why he had this perpetual attraction to Emery, especially after her stunt of looking up and applying for the same job as him. All he knew was that it existed, right there in his gut, making him jittery and warm at the same time.

They fed us dinner tonight, he told her. *Can you believe that? Jace said not to get used to it, but Elliott told me they get food a lot. I guess Belle likes to cook.*

Wow.

He noticed she hadn't said anything about her Jeep and despite him texting several more things about the ranch and asking her again about her car, she never responded again.

He eventually plugged his phone in to charge properly

and turned down the covers like a real adult. Sleep took a long time to come, mostly because he was day-dreaming about kissing Emery when she dropped him off tomorrow night.

Ridiculous ran through his mind, but still the fantasy remained.

———

Emery waited on her front porch for any sign of life from Archer's townhome. She would not make him late, and she'd set her alarm for twenty minutes earlier than she would have normally.

She yawned, her early mornings combined with her late nights catching up to her after only one day. She'd only earned one star yesterday before she'd had to leave for her job at Silver Creek.

Jace hadn't seemed too happy about her cutting out at one o'clock, but she'd explained the job at Silver Creek ended on Friday. He'd given her permission to come up to the ranch in the mornings, but she had to work in a group of three until next week, which made the opportunity for stars that much harder.

Not only that, but both of her partners were veteran cowboys, and though neither of them seemed disgruntled to be working with a woman, they hadn't been overly chatty or outgoing either.

She sipped a protein shake, the ultra-creamy texture of it almost gagging her. But she didn't think she could survive another morning of grueling physical work without a few calories in her system.

Archer's garage door finally rumbled upward, and Emery sprang from the wicker chair she kept on her front porch.

"Good morning," he said in a voice too perky for seven-thirty. "What happened to Jenny?"

He'd asked several times last night too, but she'd been too tired to explain. "She won't start."

"How did you get home?"

"One of the other counselors drove me."

"So she's over at Silver Creek?"

"Yeah." Emery took another sip of the chocolate shake and then capped it for the final time.

"I can take a look at her tonight, after you come get me."

"You don't need to."

"What are you going to do for a car?"

"I'll figure something out."

Archer nodded and pressed his foot harder on the accelerator and his mouth into a tight line. Emery sighed at herself. Why had she refused his help? She could really use it. It took the entire drive up to Horseshoe Home for her to swallow her pride.

"I could use your help," she said in a voice that was barely audible.

"Hmm?" Archer glanced at her and then the rutted road again.

"With Jenny," she said louder. "I could use your help." She hated this vulnerable feeling, this absolute helplessness.

"Sure, okay," he said easily, completely unaware of her inner turmoil over asking him. "I'll look at her tonight."

They arrived at the ranch, where it seemed like a flurry of activity was happening. "What did you do yesterday?" she asked.

"Bull pens, rope checks, and equipment repair." He grinned at her. "What about you?"

"I got calf feeding. But they're hardly calves anymore, and it was…." Hard, her mind supplied. She couldn't even imagine dealing with an adult cow. "Interesting," she finished.

He parked and practically jumped from the truck, casting her a strange look before waiting for her to join him so they could walk into the administration lodge together. Though they were fifteen minutes early, the assignment board had already been filled out and several cowboys were examining it.

Emery felt so out of place though she wore jeans like all the men, a cowboy hat like all the men, and cowboy boots like all the men. But she wasn't a man, and everyone in the room knew it. Archer got jostled as they stepped up to the board and bumped into her, his hand skating over hers.

Instant heat flamed through her whole body, and Archer's chuckle sounded hearty if not a bit nervous. "I'm with Richard today," he said, putting a few more inches between them. "I wonder who that is."

"I'm with Richard," Emery said, a frown pulling her eyebrows down.

"You are?"

She didn't like the incredulity in Archer's voice. Didn't like the way he re-checked the board as if she couldn't read.

"You two are with me," a cowboy clipped out before moving toward the exit.

"I thought we couldn't start until eight," Archer muttered under his breath. He followed anyway, a lot faster than Emery could, what with his long legs and all.

She caught up quickly and asked, "What are we doing first? I didn't have a chance to check."

Richard wore a gray cowboy hat that covered his brown hair. He glanced at her with hazel eyes as he put on a pair of leather gloves. He pulled another pair from one of his back pockets and handed them to her. "Barbed wire fence repair in the cow yard. I hope you can use a pair of wire clippers." He gave Archer a pair of gloves and he put them on before Emery could even process Richard's words.

Turned out, Emery could not use a pair of wire clippers, and every time she needed to cut an extra length of barbed wire that she'd tightened, she had to ask for help. Thankfully, Richard came to her aid each time and not Archer. But he knew, as he lifted his head toward her more often than he focused on his own work.

The job took most of the morning, and when Jace came to check it, he consulted with Richard for several seconds before saying, "Stars for Richard and Archer. Next job is in the admin lodge. Follow me."

Defeat mixed with fury in Emery's bloodstream. The urge to quit had never been so strong. She buoyed up her defenses by picturing Glenna, with her strawberry blonde hair and quick smile. If Emery didn't work, she couldn't help her sister.

As soon as she stepped into the administration lodge, she thought about maybe having Glenna come live with her instead of on her own in Spokane. Because the shenanigans happening in the administration lodge made every cell in her body scream *flight, flight!*

A ring of sorts had been defined by the desks, with a small opening near the kitchen door. One cowboy was currently on a rampage in the empty space, lowing like a cow and wearing a hat to simulate horns.

It was Ty, the foreman, and he looked like he'd been stuffed full of batteries, wound up, and then let loose.

"You're up, Caleb," the general controller said, and Caleb got up on one of the desks. He watched Ty for a few seconds, his fingers twitching and a grin stretching across his face. In the blink of an eye, he leapt into the ring, looping one arm around Ty's shoulders and pulling him to the ground in the next moment.

"Team!" the controller yelled, and a group of three men converged on a screaming, struggling Ty. One pulled up his pant leg and pinned his leg to the ground. One helped Caleb hold his head and shoulders.

The other simulated shooting something into Ty's leg.

"Time!" Caleb yelled, and all four men straightened, their eyes on the general controller.

"Eleven-point-four seconds."

A cheer went up, and Emery's stomach lurched. The

cowboys ahead of her were grouping themselves into fours, but she needed to get out of there. Fast.

"Do you guys need another person?" She glanced at the cowboy who'd come over, an inquisitive look on his face.

"Sure." Archer clapped him on the bicep like they were old friends, and the roiling in Emery's gut increased. He'd made friends here already. He fit in here. She couldn't even remember the general controller's name.

She turned to leave, but Archer took one step behind her, blocking her. His hand swept over hers, locking on and squeezing. Emery swallowed as she looked up at him, and she got lost in the intensity of his gaze as he stared down at her.

"It's okay," he said so quietly she couldn't be sure he hadn't only mouthed the words.

In the same quick motion as he'd moved and touched and talked, he slipped away like mist rising into the morning sun. There, then gone. Visible, tangible, then nothing.

"This is Elliott," he said, introducing her to the fourth cowboy who'd joined them. "Elliott, Emery. She's my next-door neighbor."

Elliott nodded at her, and he and Archer and Richard started strategizing. "I'll do the shot," she spoke up, hoping no one would argue. Of course no one did. She wasn't going to be able to tackle Ty and keep him down long enough to get the team in. She couldn't control his bucking leg and her weight wouldn't add any help to his shoulders.

One by one, the teams took their turn, but no one left

afterward. Tom kept track of the times on the assignment board, and the time to beat became 10.8 seconds with only three teams left. Emery's team stepped up to their task, and everything around her blurred.

The scent of strawberries hung in the air, mingling with the smell of men and adrenaline. Emery focused on Richard, the biggest guy in their group. He brought Ty down quickly, and the general controller yelled, "Team!"

Emery flew into the ring with the men, stabbing the "shot" in as soon as Archer had the leg secured.

"Time!" Richard called and she got to her feet, her legs shaking and the feeling of every male eye on her.

"Ten-point-nine-five," the controller called.

Emery simply turned and left the ring as Richard helped Ty get up. Elliott grinned at several of his friends, migrating toward them to give high fives. Archer stayed with her while the last two teams went.

Jace, who'd been observing all this time, pushed off of the wall and took a clipboard from Tom. He consulted the board and then the clipboards. He scratched several things on a piece of paper and handed the clipboard back to Tom.

"Team seven wins," Jace said, and whoops rent the air. "Two stars for each of them. Tom will read who else gets a star. Lunch in the kitchen. Competition resumes at one." Jace turned and went down the hall as if he didn't care about the stars, the food waiting in the kitchen, none of it. But Emery knew the man didn't miss a single thing on his ranch. A mote of dust could land on a dandelion out in a field somewhere, and Jace Lovell would know about it.

"…Emersyn Ender, Archer Bailey, Elliott Hawthorne…."

A smile burst onto Emery's face, and she turned to Archer, who wore a similar expression. "We did it." She laughed and flung herself into his arms. Instant awkwardness and regret lanced through her.

She jumped away, watching as Tom stuck a second star next to her name. Archer received his fifth, and her brief euphoria died.

Men started streaming into the kitchen, their voices and laughter so loud. Emery hung toward the back, hoping she'd go unnoticed. But in a crowd as heavily skewed toward male as this one, she couldn't expect to. So she wasn't entirely surprised when five men surrounded her, each of them smiling and congratulating her.

She caught Archer's eye, and whatever it was that existed between them sparked across the distance. He backed away, finally turning and joining the line to get food, utterly abandoning her to the other cowboys.

She wiped her hair back, feeling the pieces that had come loose from her ponytail and turned on her best smile, which admittedly, wasn't much. Still, the men around her didn't seem to detect her disinterest and maybe she could make a few friends over the course of the next few months too.

CHAPTER 5

*B*y the time Emery returned to Horseshoe Home that evening to pick up Archer, her mood had shifted from flirty and somewhat loose to tight and tired. Not only that, but Glenna had called on the way up the canyon, complaining of pain in her feet.

She always lived with some level of pain, but she'd told Emery it was worse than usual. So Emery had told her she'd call their mother, put her name on the church's prayer list, and that Glenna should call and get an appointment with the neurologist.

Archer waited on the front steps of the administration lodge, jumping up with a smile when he caught sight of her. She remained behind the wheel of his truck, and he didn't seem to mind as he folded himself onto the passenger side with a long groan.

"Rough day?" she asked.

He grinned and leaned his head against the back of the

seat. "Yeah. This afternoon, I had to load hay. Some of those guys can throw up two bales at once." He rubbed his bicep almost absently, and Emery was distracted by the bulge of his muscle beneath the fabric of his T-shirt.

She yanked her eyes away and put the truck in reverse. "I'm sort of glad I missed this afternoon then," she said. "I bet I couldn't even lift a single bale of hay, let alone throw it anywhere."

"It was tough." Archer turned his head toward her and stared. "I missed you though. Richard wasn't nearly as nice without you there." He reached across the six inches between them and took her hand in his.

Emery's first instinct was to pull her hand away, avoid the human contact. But her body sang in tune with his, and she squeezed his fingers and allowed herself to smile.

"Ah, so you do smile."

"Stop it." Her chest still felt tight, but as the miles passed, her ribs loosened.

"So do you date too?" he asked as the first twinkles of city lights came into view. She waited until she rounded the bend so she could glance at him. He wasn't looking at her, so she couldn't read his expression.

"I date," she said.

"It's just that we've lived next door to each other for two years, and I've never seen you go out with anyone."

"I'm…busy."

He chuckled. "Yeah, me too."

Emery *was* busy. She worked as much as she possibly could, which left her exhausted physically. Everything with her mother and sister made her emotionally tired, and though she craved someone to curl into at night, she simply didn't have a whole lot to give.

He let her drive through town in silence, but when she pulled into the Silver Creek parking lot, he tugged on her hand so she wouldn't get out.

"So do you want to go out with me?" he asked, looking right at her, those smoky, dark eyes peering at her through the twilight.

Surprise danced through her, even more so when she heard herself say, "Sure. I'd like that."

———

Archer's insides didn't want to settle back into their proper places after Emery said she'd go out with him. He'd grinned and gotten out of the truck quickly so he wouldn't say anything else or act like a goofball.

"All right," he said, exhaling. "Let's see what we've got goin' on with Jenny." He pointed to the driver's side door. "You want to pop the hood?"

Emery did, and Archer stared down into the dirty engine. He couldn't help thinking that his father would know exactly what to do, almost like the machine spoke to him, whispered where it hurt and leaked.

Unfortunately, Archer didn't quite possess the same mechanical instinct. But he knew how to check the battery, the spark plugs, the fluid levels. "She's out of oil," he said.

"Oh, I have some in the back."

"Does she leak a lot?" He wiped his hands on a blue rag from the back of his truck.

"Yeah." Emery handed him a bottle of motor oil and held another at her side. He set to work getting everything filled and checked while she ate an apple and watched from his tailgate. She had to get back to work, and Archer let himself watch her walk away, the swing of her hips as enticing to him as the sadness in her soul.

He went to the automotive store and got more oil, washer fluid, and antifreeze. Jenny was as dry as a fossil, and she seemed to sigh in relief as he poured bottles of liquid into her tanks. He checked her plugs and they looked okay. He replaced the starter, and put a gasoline cleaner in her tank, his credit card taking a fifty-dollar hit.

Archer didn't care. He couldn't stand to feel the worry in Emery, not when he could do something to help.

Before he tried starting Jenny, he hooked the jumper cables from his truck to her battery. When he sat behind the wheel, he bowed his head and said, "Please, Lord. She can't afford this right now."

He couldn't either, because his next call would have to be to his father.

He wrenched the key, the prayer steadily running through his mind. The engine roared to life, and Archer jumped from the seat, a cry of triumph rising into the sky.

He grabbed a napkin from his glove box and wrote a quick note to Emery. *Jenny runs! Come see me when you get home.*

He stuck it under her windshield wiper on the driver's side and left her keys under the floor mat. He really wanted to stop by a fast food restaurant on his way home, but he bypassed one after the other, the meager amount in his checking account preventing him from making an unwise decision.

At home, he fed Carrot Cake and let him out to take care of his business. Then he showered, the pain in his head not nearly as intense tonight as it had been last night. He entered the kitchen, with his towel around his neck and wearing only a pair of basketball shorts. He pulled out the loaf of bread and the peanut butter jar and put together a double decker sandwich for dinner.

He'd taken one bite when someone rapped on his door. Carrot started yapping, his high-pitched bark nowhere near scary enough to ward anyone off.

"Just a sec," Archer called, abandoning the sandwich in favor of the bedroom, where he pulled a clean shirt over his head. When he pulled open the door, Emery stood there, fresh from Silver Creek.

She beamed at him. "You fixed Jenny."

He laughed. "You've got to keep her hydrated, especially driving up the canyon all the time."

She leaned her hip into the doorway as Carrot Cake put his front paws on her knees. She reached down and scratched the little dog, and Archer licked his lips, tasting peanut butter but smelling a hint of her tantalizing raspberry and brown sugar scent underneath the sweat, horse, and sky she also brought with her. He found all of it sexy, and he couldn't believe this was the woman who'd lived next door for so long.

"You want to come in?" he asked.

"I was thinking," she said as she passed him and entered his house. He suddenly worried what it smelled like. "We're both going to be going up to the ranch for the next few months. Seems silly for both of us to drive."

"Totally silly." He let his fingers casually brush hers as he retrieved his peanut butter sandwich from the counter.

"I really am sorry about this job," she said, her eyes bright blue and soft at the same time. "I'm not going to get it, but it's four months of work I need."

He chewed and swallowed, his eyes never leaving hers. "Why do you need the job so badly?"

"Same as you." She folded her arms.

Archer cocked his head. "Yeah, I don't think so. You've been working for three months straight, and I know the salary they paid you at Silver Creek. You should be doing fine."

She met his eyes with fear in hers. "I help my sister out."

His eyebrows rose. "Is she older or younger?"

"Younger. She was in an accident when she was nine years old, and she's paralyzed from the waist down. She can't work much. She does what she can, and she lives on her own. Pays for her own apartment." Emery lifted her chin. "My mother works three jobs just to get by herself, and we're all just doin' the best we can."

Archer polished off his sandwich. "I understand." And he really wanted her to stop talking. He'd suspected she had a story like this one, and while he'd thought he wanted to hear it, he found he didn't.

Because it made his heart soften toward her when it was practically melted already. How could he compete against her now? The gentlemanly side of him wanted to make sure *she* got the job come Christmas, but the practical side of him screamed that *he* needed this job—just as much as her, though in a different way.

"What about you?" Emery leaned against the counter.

"You want to sit?" He chin nodded toward the sofa in the living room. "We don't have to stand."

She followed him the few steps into the living room, and sat facing him on the couch. Carrot Cake took his spot on the floor, a doleful look at Emery.

"You look different without your cowboy hat." She grinned and extended her hand toward him like she might touch him. Her arm dropped at the last moment. "Younger."

He didn't quite know what to say, so he just said, "Thanks," and stuffed his hands under his arms to keep himself from manhandling her. "And I need this job so my father will see me as a real man."

Emery's nose scrunched up, and Archer found it downright cute. "What does that mean?"

"It means I've disappointed him in a lot of ways, and I need this job to actually turn into a career so I can prove to him that I'm not...like him."

All at once, his father's antagonistic behavior made crystal clear sense in Archer's mind. His father had bounced from job to job, doing what he could to keep the lights on and food on the table. And he simply wanted better for his sons.

"And you want to be a career cowboy?"

"Yes," Archer said without a moment's hesitation. "I love working outside. I love animals. I like using my hands."

Emery ducked her head and put one of her hands in his. "You have nice hands." Her words dove into Archer's chest and embedded themselves in his heart. She traced her fingertip along his palm, which tickled, and along his pinkie.

Snaps and pops exploded through his body, and his blood ran a little faster. He squeezed her hand and chuckled. "Stop it."

"Ticklish?"

"Oh, yeah. My feet are the worst though."

A mischievous glint entered her eye, and Archer wondered when he'd entered this weird place where Emery came over after work and hung out with him. Where he held her hand, where the possibility of kissing her was very, very real.

He ducked his head to somehow hide his thoughts, aware of how silly that sounded. He lifted her hand to his lips and said, "We can ride together tomorrow. Want me to drive?"

She shook her head, the blonde tips of her ponytail brushing her shoulders. "No, I still have to work at Silver Creek for another couple of days. We can start the carpool next week."

"On Saturday," he corrected. "Six days a week, holidays included, until Christmas."

Emery groaned and her eyes fell closed. "I was hoping to sleep in on Saturday."

Archer laughed. "Please, you don't sleep in."

She narrowed her eyes at him. "What?"

"I hear you over there at like, seven o'clock in the morning, opening drawers or something."

Surprise flitted across her face. "You can hear me opening drawers?"

"I think your bathroom butts up against mine."

"I can hear you blending stuff." She rested her head in her free hand, a measure of exhaustion coming through in her expression. "At least it sounds like a blender. One of those ultra-expensive ones."

"I won it in a raffle," he said. "And I do use it every morning. Sorry, I didn't know it was that loud."

She gave him a soft smile, one he imagined crossing her face in the moments before she fell asleep, or in that heartbeat just as he was about to kiss her. His heart pumped out an extra beat and he said, "You should get on home and get some rest. You look tired."

"Just what every girl wants to hear." She giggled and pushed herself off his couch. "See you tomorrow, Archer."

CHAPTER 6

Archer hurried through his morning routine, determined to leave for the ranch before Emery. If he was going to let her win some contests and stars at the ranch, he certainly couldn't have her beating him to work.

Sure enough, he pulled in a full five minutes before she did, satisfaction singing through him. He didn't see her as his assigned partner for the day was none other than Ty Barker, the foreman at the ranch.

Nerves cascaded through Archer like a waterfall as Ty led him toward the horse barn. "So in here, we make sure the equipment is put away properly; we check the horse's hooves, and all the stalls need to be mucked out." He turned and walked backward, a grin reaching all the way into his eyes. "It's the best place to sneak a kiss, if you have a girl up here at the ranch."

Archer tipped his head back and sent a laugh into the sky. "How many women are actually up here?"

"Available women?" Ty glanced around like he was really trying to take stock. "Just one, I reckon."

"Who's that?"

"That gorgeous blonde that was on your team yesterday."

"Emery?"

"Yeah, Emery." Ty gave him a sideways look. "Are you and her together?"

Archer thought about his recent kissing fantasies and the real life version of holding her hand. "Nah, we just live next door to each other." He wondered what Ty had seen that made him think Archer and Emery were dating.

"Oh, the woman next door. That can be awesome."

"She's got a lot going on in her life."

Ty's expression clouded, but his sunny disposition broke through quick enough. "Don't we all."

And Archer supposed everyone did.

The next couple of days passed with more ranch work being learned, his muscles getting used to the constant physical labor, and private competitions between him and Emery that only Archer knew about. He won every one of them, and he'd given himself so many mental gold stars he'd earned himself a prize.

That happened to be a hamburger on Friday after he finished working on the ranch, coupled with a car ride up the canyon with Emery on Saturday morning. Out of the five cowboys up for the job, Archer was in the early lead. He tried not to let it go to his head. Instead, he put his head down and worked as hard as he could, listened to the cowboys he got paired with, and enjoyed the home cooked meals whenever they were available.

After a few weeks, his body had acclimated to his new schedule and adapted to the physical exertion required to be a career cowboy. His bank account had a little extra padding, and he treated himself to a hamburger and fries every Friday evening.

He'd made friends with several of the cowboys at the ranch, especially Elliott, and they sat next to one another at church. A few more employees of Horseshoe Home usually filled the bench, with Emery down at the end.

He still hadn't taken her out on that date, as she didn't seem to have much energy for such activities. He'd asked her a few more questions about her sister, and Emery opened up to him when they spent time alone. As soon as they arrived at Horseshoe Home though, she cut off all the smiles and hand-holding and got down to business.

By the time October rolled around, she was in fourth place among the new cowboys, but neither of them were anywhere near the top of the charts. Caleb Chamberlain had claimed that spot early on, and he wasn't giving it up. Archer suspected his best friend—who happened to be Ty —was giving him double stars. But he watched as Tom stuck them on for the day, and Caleb only got one for each win.

"No work this weekend," Jace said one Wednesday evening. "It's the Spooktacular, and we all need a break."

Half of the men groaned and half cheered. Archer, who now sat in the middle of the pack star-wise, was relieved.

He hadn't worked six days a week, from sunup to practically sundown in, well, ever.

He enjoyed the work, just as he'd told Emery, but the relentless way Mother Nature seemed to undo all of their hard work every day, only to require them to perform it again, could be exhausting.

Archer edged through the crowd until he stood just behind Emery. He leaned forward and whispered, "Dinner on Saturday night?"

She twisted to look at him, a light in her eyes she tried to mask unsuccessfully. "Sh," she said with a smile.

Archer settled against the wall and folded his arms, a smile accompanying him while the boss continued with the schedule and directions. Jace dismissed the men after a recap of the standings, and Emery slipped away from Archer among all the bodies. Didn't matter. He'd driven that morning.

Sure enough, she sat on his tailgate, her long legs swinging as she watched him approach. His heart thundered in his chest and he pushed himself up to join her. "Dinner on Saturday night?" he asked again.

"Sure." She faced him for half a second. "Where do you want to go?"

He hadn't actually thought that far ahead. He only knew he'd asked her out almost two months ago and they'd never gone. "Wherever you want."

"The Spooktacular has a big food truck rally," she said. "We could go to that, wander around the craft fair or something."

He grinned at her. It was the "or something" he'd been dreaming about.

———

Emery wasn't sure what was happening with her and Archer. He'd asked her out, but then never followed through. They spent a lot of time together as they drove to and from the ranch. He held her hand every day, and they spent an hour or so together in the evenings.

But they didn't go out. They didn't sit together at church the way most couples did. He didn't do more than hold her hand, ever. No hugging, not even a little peck on her cheek. And she was starting to get frustrated.

She understood that they worked a lot, and neither of them had much money to go out very often. But she wanted a clearer line on where they stood, if she could kiss him whenever she wanted to, if they could hold hands outside the privacy of their cars.

Saturday night finally arrived, and Emery shimmied into her skinny jeans and put on a pink sweatshirt to ward off the near-winter chill. She slipped on her cowgirl boots with the pink stitching just as Archer knocked on the door and opened it. "Hey, there." His gaze scanned her from the top of her head to the soles of her boots, practically devouring her.

She turned in a slow circle and held her arms out. "Festive enough?"

He laughed as he drew closer, the spark of desire she'd seen in his eyes ramping up to a full-fledged flame. "Not even close," he said. "You realize most people will be wearing black or orange, right?" He fingered the sleeve of her sweatshirt and swallowed, a nervous gesture she'd seen several men do before talking to her.

Not that she'd dated much over the course of the past eight years. She had boyfriends in high school, but once she'd graduated, her responsibility to help Glenna had descended on her with the weight of a freight train.

She'd had lots of interest, sure, but word got around town that Emersyn Ender didn't date, and the men had dried up. Archer obviously hadn't gotten that memo, and Emery didn't want him to get it.

"This is pink," he said, his voice strained.

"I like pink."

His fingers moved from her shirtsleeve to the ends of her curls. Though he wasn't touching her skin, or her clothes, the intimacy between them jumped up a notch. "I like pink too." Archer's eyes drifted closed for a moment as he leaned closer and inhaled the scent of her skin. The brim of his cowboy hat bumped against her collarbone, and he took it off.

"I like it when *you* wear pink," he whispered. His lips briefly touched her neck, and Emery had never felt such a sizzle. She'd frozen to the floor. The nearness of him made her head swim, and before she knew it, she'd reached up and put her arms on his shoulders.

"We should go, don't you think?" His husky voice only made her want to stay, to define that line so she'd have a clear idea of what they were.

She reined in her feelings and stuffed them back into the hole where she'd kept them for so long. Emery moved toward the front door and opened it at the same time a terrific crash of thunder ripped through the sky.

Stepping onto the porch, she peered into the cosmos. Archer pressed up close behind her, both of his hands landing on her waist. She enjoyed this game, these soft touches and slow advances. She'd been on the dating bench for a while, but it felt good to be playing again.

"Maybe we should order pizza," he said.

"I really want one of those foot-long corndogs." She twisted and peered up into his handsome face. "Please?"

"I can make you a corndog in my oven. It's going to snow tonight."

"Let's go quick then." She jangled her keys. "Jenny loves the snow."

He chuckled and gestured her down the steps. She drove over to the recreation center, where the food trucks had pulled into a tight circle so their awnings would protect customers. Hardly anyone had come, and Emery felt bad for the restaurant owners outside and the small businesses set up inside the building.

She got her corndog. Archer ordered one too, as well as a huge platter of curly fries. The wind whistled, and Archer turned toward her. "Can we go now?"

She took a big bite of her corndog and nodded. They'd made it about halfway back to her house when the first flakes of snow fell. Emery flipped on Jenny's windshield wipers and exclaimed over the weather.

"You like snow?" Archer asked.

"Would I live in Montana if I didn't like snow?" She giggled, happier than she'd been in a long, long time. She purposefully didn't pull into her garage, all of her brain power focused on one thing: a kiss with Archer in the snow.

"What—?"

She jumped from Jenny and went out onto their shared front lawn, her arms spread wide, her head tipped back, the magic of the first snow of the season obviously infectious, because Archer joined her.

He laughed and twirled her around, bringing her back against his body. Archer swayed with her, gazing into her eyes. She closed hers and enjoyed the cold touch of snowflakes on her skin.

His warm hands cradled her face, and she opened her eyes only to dive right into the depths of his. "Emery," he whispered.

She didn't know what he was going to say, but she couldn't wait any longer. She lifted up on her toes and pressed her lips to his. He only seemed startled for a second, and then he kissed her properly, his mouth moving in tandem with hers so effortlessly, so wonderfully.

True, Emery hadn't been kissed in a while, but she was sure none of them had been this spectacular. She breathed in the masculine scent of his cologne, smiled against his lips, and kissed him again.

CHAPTER 7

Several days later, Emery's phone rang before she'd gotten out of bed. Glenna's name came up on the caller ID, and concern spiked Emery's pulse.

"Glenna?"

"Sorry to call so early."

"It's fine." Emery swung her feet over the side of the bed, a chill in the early morning darkness she definitely didn't like about winter. "What's going on?"

"I'm in the hospital."

Emery's vision faded to white, and she blinked to bring it back. "Are you okay?"

"My wheelchair skidded on the ice as I was going into work this morning." She cleared her throat, the tears she was crying evident in the thickness of her voice. "I fell onto my side, and it took three people to get me upright. My whole right side is bruised, and I'm going to be here for a few days." Soft sniffles and sobs came through the speaker. "I'm sorry, Emery."

"It's not your fault, Glenna." Emery ran her fingers through her hair, trying to think. "I have to work today, but I'll figure something out." Her mind raced along the two-hour route to Spokane, the canyons and winding roads, the construction. Maybe she could talk to Jace, get a few days off.

She wasn't going to win the contest, that much had been made clear in the first week. But work was work, and she believed that doors would open if she put forth her best efforts and made the right connections.

The phone conversation lasted several more minutes, with Emery soothing Glenna until she felt like her sister had stopped crying. Emery had dressed during the call, and she hurried downstairs to put on her boots.

It was early—before seven still—but she went next door and knocked anyway. She paced away from Archer's door, down the one step to the lawn, and back. She'd completed the circuit four times before a fresh-from-bed Archer opened the door.

She stared at him, struck dumb by his handsomeness—which seemed stupid really. She saw him every day. Had been kissing him before work and after work for a solid week. But this softer, rumpled version of Archer was so sexy Emery couldn't even make her body do its involuntary functions.

"What's wrong?" he asked, rubbing a hand through his messy hair. Emery wanted to do the same.

She shook her hormone-driven thoughts away. She was here about her sister. She needed help with Glenna.

"My sister needs me for a few days," she managed to say though her throat felt like she'd swallowed cotton. "I'm going to call Jace and see if he'll give me a few days off."

Archer stepped out onto his tiny porch and drew her into his chest. Warmth emanated through the thin fabric of his shirt, and she inhaled deeply to commit the scent of him to memory. He was strong, and secure, and kind. Everything Emery wanted in her life. She'd enjoyed so much being able to have someone to talk to at night. And she was certain he was the best kisser in the whole state of Montana.

Her heart flopped in her chest, torn between him and Glenna. She didn't exactly know when she'd given any of it to him, but she definitely had.

"I can talk to him if you just need to go," Archer whispered, stroking her hair with one hand and pressing her into his body with gentle pressure against her back with the other.

Emery held onto him like she was drowning. "No, I can do it. I just wanted to let you know that I can't drive today."

He pulled back and looked into her eyes. A soft smile, filled with adoration, crossed his face. He tucked her hair behind her ear. "All right. Call me when you get to Spokane? I worry about Jenny on that road."

She kissed him, pouring all her concern, her fear, into the gesture. He gladly took it, deepening their connection until she thought sure her body would combust from the slow, passionate heat of his mouth.

He pulled away roughly, his chest heaving. "Sorry," he murmured, backing up a step.

But Emery wanted more. Not less. Not an apology. She put distance between them too, though, retreating from the porch as her hazed mind tried to reason. The chill in the November air helped, and she regained her control.

Archer wore an air of embarrassment, but he kept his gaze on hers.

"I should go," Emery said.

He nodded, folding his arms across his chest as if cold. He probably was as he only wore that T-shirt and a pair of gym shorts. She returned to him, pressed a chaste kiss to his soft mouth, and said, "I'll call you when I get to Spokane."

She turned and went around the divider separating their front doors. Once inside the safety of her own house, she dialed Jace. He answered on the first ring, and she marveled that the man never seemed to sleep.

"Jace, it's Emersyn Ender. I have a problem with my sister…."

———

Driving up to the ranch alone after two months of sharing the ride with Emery felt like torture to Archer. He'd pulled out her garbage can though it was only Tuesday and he'd stood in her garage, his mind circling that kiss on his front porch.

He'd gone too far, and he knew it. She hadn't seemed to mind; it felt like she even wanted to push it farther. But she was distressed, not in her right mind, and Archer knew better anyway.

He pulled into the ranch, which held a skiff of snow on the ground, and went into the administration lodge. Elliott rose from a desk and gestured for Archer to come over. He did, taking a chair from a nearby desk and twisting it to face his friend.

"What's wrong with Emery?"

"Nothing," Archer said. "Her sister needed her in Spokane." He studied Elliott, who didn't seem like a gossipy man. "How did you know?"

"Jace called an early staff meeting and told us. Asked us to pray for her."

Something touched Archer's heart. The cowboys here really were family, and he wanted to be here so badly his throat burned. The fire moved into his chest, singeing everything it touched.

A voice whispered that he should call his mother and get across town to see his own family. Today.

Elliott stood. "C'mon. You're with me today."

Confusion shot through Archer. "I am? Why?"

"Jace wanted you to have an easy day, what with Emery's situation and all." He was acting like Emery had died or something.

Archer glanced around, and the ranch definitely had a more somber feeling today. He felt melancholy himself, only because of the intense worry in his gut. *Help Jenny make it to Spokane,* he prayed as Elliott said, "There're doughnuts in the kitchen."

After properly carb-loading, Archer spent the day working with the cattle they'd brought down from the upper fields. They'd spend the winter closer to the ranch's epicenter, and they all needed to be accounted for.

The work was easy, if tedious, but also brought with it a heavy amount of cow dung. Archer thought he'd never get the smell out of his nose—or his clothes. Even Carrot Cake, who usually greeted him with a doggie smile and a wagging tail, retreated to the kitchen when Archer got home.

Emery hadn't called, and worry seethed in his gut. Every time someone at the ranch had asked, he'd felt like throwing up. At first, he'd thought it was because he didn't get great service up the canyon, but his phone still sat silent, no texts or missed calls coming through.

He plugged in the device and restarted it before going to shower. Finally clean and smelling more like a pine forest than a dung heap, he checked his phone.

Still nothing.

So Archer perched on the edge of his bed, his hair still dripping a little onto his bare shoulders, and called Emery. She didn't answer, which didn't exactly help the parade of animals moving through his stomach. His chest tightened, an invisible band of pressure threatening to cut off his air supply.

He was trying to figure out what to do next—jump in his truck and make the two-hour drive himself? Call his mom right now? Get down on his knees and pray?—when his phone rang.

"Emery," he breathed into the phone. "I've been so worried."

"I'm sorry I didn't call." She sounded like she was two light years away, not two hours. "I've had spotty service all day, and meetings with doctors, and I just realized that all my texts to you never went through."

"You sound—how are things going?" She didn't need to hear that she sounded stressed, harried, tired.

"Glenna is okay," she said. "She'll be here for a few days while they make sure she's healing up right." She paused, but Archer didn't fill the silence. He sensed Emery had more to say.

"I'm bringing her home with me," she finally said. "She's in a lot of pain, and now she's terrified to go into work." Emery sighed, and not the happy blissful kind he'd heard her do after he'd kissed her. "So I'm going to go through her apartment and see what I can fit in Jenny. We'll see if we can sell her apartment lease. And she'll live with me until she figures out what to do next."

Archer's heart hurt for his girlfriend. "What can I do to help?"

"Well." She cleared her throat, and all the emotion in that single word indicated that she was crying. The tense silence coming through the line confirmed it.

Archer wanted to be there with her so badly. He should've gone with her, and a rush of anger at himself flowed through him. "Hey, it's all right," he said quietly. "Okay, Em? It's all right. What do you need?"

Sniffling came through the line, and Archer's heart

cracked. "I can be there in two hours. Let me pack a bag." He stood, realizing he wasn't even dressed.

"No," she said. "It's three hours with the blasted road construction. You don't need to come." She drew in a breath that shuddered even over the phone. "I'm going to need a lot of help with Glenna. She can't navigate stairs."

Understanding bloomed in Archer's mind. "And all our bedrooms are upstairs."

"Right."

"I can carry her," he said. "I don't know if you've noticed, but I'm *pretty* strong these days." He smiled, hoping his bragging had prompted a smile from her too. "I mean, I can almost lift two hay bales now, just like some of the other cowboys."

"Oh, I've noticed."

He laughed, glad some of the seriousness was lifting. "So hurry up and bring Glenna home," he said. "I miss you."

"I miss you too," she said, causing Archer's spirits to soar. She certainly kissed him like she liked him, and he marveled that their friendship had morphed into something more so quickly—especially after she'd done something that had made him so angry.

But working with her up at the ranch had been…nice. A comfort, actually, even though he got along really great with everyone and enjoyed the work.

He got dressed and called his mother, the idea of her sweet and sour meatballs on his mind. She'd probably have a pot of soup on the stove though. She liked to make stews and chowders when the weather turned bad.

"Archer," she said with a heavy dose of surprise in her voice. "How are you? How's the ranch?"

"Great, Mom," he said, his soul brightening. "Just great."

"A couple more months until you know about the job, right?"

"Right." He swallowed. "I was thinking of coming over tonight. My girlfriend—"

His mom sucked in a breath and then let out a squeal. "Archie! You have a girlfriend? Why haven't I heard this before?"

Archer rolled his eyes. He should've known not to mention Emery. There would be questions and side-glances with his father, and Archer wouldn't be able to leave the house until his mother had been satisfied—and that could take hours.

At the same time, he wanted the world to know that he was with Emery, a gorgeous, thoughtful, hardworking woman who made him happier than he'd been, well, ever.

In that moment, with his mother still gushing and asking who she was, Archer realized that maybe, just maybe, he'd started to fall in love with Emery. Fear gripped his heart and squeezed, only because Archer didn't know what love felt like. Not really.

He'd never had a serious girlfriend, always thinking himself unworthy of one. After all, he had no way to provide a life for himself, let alone a woman or children. His father had taught him that, at least.

"So are you coming?" his mom asked, and Archer realized he'd missed everything she'd said.

Didn't matter. He had a glow in his chest, all because of Emery.

"Yeah," he said. "I'll be right over."

Apprehension knotted the muscles in his shoulders when he pulled into his parents' driveway. The windows shone with yellow light, creating a cheery atmosphere Archer knew only extended to one member in the house. His father would acknowledge him, perhaps even carry on a civil conversation about the weather or the upcoming Thanksgiving holiday.

But inevitably, his dad would say something pointed, jagged, meant to hurt Archer. He gathered his wits and thought about what Xan, his NASA-employed brother, had told him.

"It's not that he's trying to hurt you, Arch. He just wants you to understand that your choices have consequences."

Archer had argued with Xan that of course he knew his choices had consequences. The fact that he lived paycheck to paycheck when his brothers didn't testified of that. Archer didn't need his dad to point it out every single time they got together, because all that did was force Archer to stay away.

He opened the screen door and went inside, calling, "Hey, Mom. Dad?"

His mom came bustling down the hall and into the main living area, which merged seamlessly into the kitchen and dining area. His father had done all the home improvements during times when he wasn't working. They didn't have a huge house, or even the nicest materials inside, but it was clean and open and Archer felt something stir in him that had long gone dormant.

He hugged his mother, realizing it was her he missed. Her he should make more of an effort to involve in his life. If his dad wanted to be prickly, fine, but his mom had never been anything but supportive.

"Smells good in here."

"Corn and cheese chowder," she said. "And I threw in some bread just before you called, so it should be out soon." She held onto his arms and looked up into his face, happiness and hope shining in her eyes. "It's so good to see you. You look…bigger."

"I've gained a few muscles working around the ranch," he said.

She gestured for him to enter the kitchen, and they sat at the bar together. "So you like the ranch?"

That spark of hope, that ultimate longing, pulled through him. "Mom, it's so great. I really hope I get the job up there. The cowboys get a cabin, Mom. A house to live in, right on-site. They treat each other like family. The owner is great, and there are a few ranch wives that feed the cowboys sometimes." He sighed, realizing everything he'd ever wanted sat up at Horseshoe Home. "I really want the job. It could be my career."

"What's your plan if you don't get it?"

Archer swung toward the sound of his father's voice. He had the same black hair, the same overgrown eyebrows, the same stance as Archer when he folded his arms—like he was now.

"I'm going to get it, Dad," Archer said. The timer on the oven read twenty-four minutes. Twenty-four minutes before the bread would even be done.

"But what if you don't?"

"There are three other ranches up the canyon, and I have experience now. I know what to do. I'm employable on any ranch, anywhere. I'll find something." Archer marveled at the confidence in his voice, his heart, his soul. Though his dad had never shown him that same confidence, Archer possessed it. He wondered where it came from.

"Dave," his mother said.

"What? I'm just askin' the boy some questions."

"I'm not a boy, Dad." Archer exhaled, not wanting to fight tonight.

"Tell us about your girlfriend," his mom said, getting up to stir the chowder.

Archer didn't really want to talk about that either, but he had come here to talk. He'd been *led* here, and he didn't want to disappoint the Lord by being petty. So he told them about Emery, his words becoming more animated and the strength in him increasing.

"So she's working up at the ranch too," his dad said.

"Yep, that's right."

"So she could get the job you want."

"She's not going to get it, Dad."

"How do you know?"

"Because I just do." He didn't want to explain the whole star chart to his parents. His dad wouldn't understand it anyway.

He'd want to know how a job could be earned with stickers, and why didn't Jace just give the job to who he thought was the best? Archer would try to explain that the stickers proved who was best, but his dad simply wouldn't get it.

"But it's a possibility."

"Sure, Dad. It's a possibility." The timer went off for the bread, and Archer thanked the Lord for that. The conversation stalled as bowls and spoons were set out, and bread sliced, and chowder served. His father said grace, and Archer was struck with how powerful his father's faith was. He'd never truly noticed that before, but it bled through in the words of his prayer so forcefully that Archer had to listen.

They ate, mostly in silence, another small miracle Archer expressed mental gratitude for. He answered his mom's questions about Emery, and the ranch, and anything else she wanted to know. "You're eating okay?" She always asked that.

"Mom, you just said you thought I looked better." He grinned and chuckled. "I'm eating great."

He helped her clean up the dishes, aware of his father's watchful eyes. He didn't want to stick around to hear what was brewing in his dad's brain, so he said, "I should go. Work on the ranch starts before the sun gets up." He grinned and hugged his mother again.

His dad followed him to the front door and they shared a quick embrace. "Work hard, son," he said just before Archer stepped into the cold. Archer wanted to tell him how hard he'd been working, but he just walked down the sidewalk, got in his truck, and went on home.

His father of all people should know that sometimes hard work didn't win the race. Maybe that was what he'd meant, which only added fuel to the frustrated fire simmering in Archer's bloodstream. He could have the most stars and still not get this job, something he'd never considered before tonight.

But Jace was a person, and maybe he *would* hire Emery if he thought she needed the job more than Archer did. After all, families took care of each other, right?

His competitive spirit flared to life. *He* needed this job. Badly. And he needed to make sure Jace knew it.

CHAPTER 8

$\mathcal{A}$rcher went under the Double-H ranch sign early the next morning. He parked and got out of his truck, his breath hanging in the air in front of him. It must have been fate, or serendipity, or maybe the hand of God, because Jace was crossing the lane to the administration lodge at that very moment.

"You're here early," he said to Archer.

"Yeah," he said. "Didn't have to wait for Emery, and I couldn't sleep in. So I just came up. Figured I could nurse my coffee here as well as at home."

Jace nodded. "You live alone." He wasn't asking.

"Yep." Archer usually didn't mind being alone, but after experiencing the joy and wonder and love here at the ranch, he realized he wouldn't want to be alone forever. "I have a little dog. He keeps me company sometimes, but he's been in a depression since Emery left." He chuckled. "Somehow, he got all attached to her."

Jace climbed the steps and held open the door for Archer. "That can happen."

Archer stepped past him and turned back when he saw the front area was vacant. "I just wanted to thank you for this job. I mean, I know I don't have it, but I'm really hoping I'll get it. I've wanted to be a cowboy for a long time."

Jace appraised him, and Archer let him look. "What else have you done?" Jace continued toward the kitchen where someone had already started the coffee.

"A little bit of everything. Worked in a restaurant as a line cook. Worked for the city for a summer in the parks and rec department. Even tried my hand at fixing cars. This is the best fit for me." He felt it, way down deep in his soul. The familiar desperation he'd become friends with over the past few months lodged in his throat.

"Well, you're a good cowboy," Jace said. "Leading the recruits on the star chart, aren't you?"

"Yes, sir."

Jace grinned and sipped his coffee. "I'm sure you'll have your career one way or another." He nodded and left the kitchen, going down the hall and into his office, where he closed the door.

Archer stood in the kitchen, holding his coffee mug, numb. That conversation hadn't gone exactly how he'd wanted it to. In his daydreams, Jace offered him the job on the spot, saying he was the best cowboy of the hirees, and Horseshoe Home simply couldn't survive without him.

This version wasn't nearly as rewarding, but a little niggle of hope remained in his gut. Jace knew who he was.

He knew where he sat on the chart. Maybe his father's advice to keep working hard would pay off in the end.

Elliott entered the kitchen and said, "It's so cold out there already." He poured himself a mug full of coffee. "Ranching in the winter isn't so much fun."

"I don't think it's so bad," Archer said.

"You haven't done it yet." Elliott grinned. "I really hope you get this job so I can see how you deal with ten-foot snow drifts in February." He seemed almost giddy about such a thing.

Archer laughed. "I bet I've done worse." He sobered, because he knew what was worse. Having no job at all.

———

"Okay, here we are." Emery eased Jenny over the bump in her driveway, going as slow as she could so she didn't jostle Glenna too much. Her poor sister had pain in her spine from the fall, and if she could feel her legs, she'd probably be worse than she was.

Emery didn't pull into the garage but left Jenny idling just shy of it. "Stay here. I'll go get Archer." She'd told Glenna all about Archer, that she couldn't steal him away from Emery just because he was going to sweep her off her feet and carry her into the house.

Glenna had rolled her eyes and laughed. She'd said, "Men don't look at me, Emery," in a really vulnerable voice that had pulled on Emery's heartstrings. She found her sister beautiful, with the same gold-spun hair she had, the same crystal-blue eyes. The only difference was the wheelchair, really, and she prayed as she jogged up to Archer's door that he would be able to see the beauty in her sister.

Her phone rang, and she answered it with, "Hey, Mom. We just pulled in."

"I'm on my way. I have dinner."

Emery's stomach growled and then clenched. "Sounds great. See you soon." She knocked on Archer's door and hung up her phone. Her mother was a good mom, doing the best she could with decades-old medical bills still plaguing her. A sting of resentment for the father she hadn't spoken to in twenty years accompanied the warm feelings about her mom.

Archer pulled open the door and said, "Hey, you," before gathering her into his arms. She exhaled, so glad to be back in Gold Valley, back with him.

He kissed her, the depth of his feelings plain to experience with his gentle touch that seemed powerful at the same time.

"My mom's on her way over, and we need help getting Glenna inside."

He flexed his muscles. "I know what I'm good for."

She laughed, though she thought he was good for a lot more than just eye candy. He soothed her, ironed out her wrinkled thoughts, and made her want to be a better person. She undid her ponytail and re-secured it tightly as they walked over to Jenny.

Emery opened her sister's door. "Glenna, this is Archer Bailey. He's my next-door neighbor and my boyfriend.

Remember how you're not going to charm him away from me?"

Archer laughed and volleyed his gaze from Emery to Glenna. "I don't know, Emery. You might be beat here." He extended his hand to Glenna to shake, and Emery saw a real smile on her sister's face, something she hadn't seen in a long time.

"Nice to meet you," she said, making a feeble attempt with her good arm to scoot herself further out of the car.

"Don't do that, Glenna," Emery said at the same time Archer said, "I'll get you, Glenna. Don't you worry." In one swift movement, he lifted her out of the Jeep, smiling the whole time.

"Oh, you're as light as a feather." He chuckled and took Glenna up the salted sidewalk. Emery noticed the way the dusting of snow had been removed on her side, the pink cubes of salt Archer had ensured were in place for their arrival.

Her heart swelled once, twice, three times its normal size. She pushed the passenger door closed and gathered two bags from the back seat before following the man who was acting like her personal savior. Tears gathered behind her eyes, making her whole head hot.

Archer had settled Glenna on the couch, her legs extended in front of her onto an ottoman, with a blanket over her. She sighed. "That's fine, Archer. I think this is best for my back right now."

"Mom's almost here," Emery said, setting the bags at the bottom of the stairs.

"What else do you need from Jenny?" Archer asked, striding to her side. His fingers touched hers, a dance the ten of them performed together before he claimed her hand and squeezed it. "You okay?" he whispered.

She nodded, one of her tears splashing her cheek. She wiped it away quickly. "This is all we need for tonight. Glenna has more things in the back, but we can get them later."

"I can put stuff wherever you need," he said. He used his free hand to guide her eyes to his. "Let me help you. Please."

Emery had boxed up all her emotions and stored them on a shelf in the back of her mind. Glenna needed her to be strong. Glenna needed her to be in charge. Glenna needed her.

But with Archer, she could be weak. She could cry. She could let him shoulder some of the burden.

"Glenna." Archer strode back to the couch. "We'll be right back, okay? Will you be okay here?"

"Fine," Glenna said, a note of weariness in her voice.

Archer returned to where Emery stood, her emotions spilling out everywhere. "Come on, sweetheart." He tucked her into his side and took her to his house next door. He sat on the couch and she curled into his side, her tears staining his T-shirt. He simply let her cry, his breathing even and calm, an anchor for her in her personal storm.

Several long minutes later, she calmed enough for him to say, "She seems nice."

"She is nice."

He stroked her hair and held her close, the tenderness

with which he handled her welcome and wanted. How he knew how to deal with women, she didn't know. He didn't have any sisters, and he'd claimed not to have had any serious girlfriends.

"You want some hot chocolate?" he asked.

She smiled through her continuing sniffles. "Sure."

"My mother always made hot chocolate when I was upset." He spoke in a hushed, almost reverent voice. "I've learned that it usually makes everything better."

She gazed up at him, a sense of love infecting her, swirling through her. She'd lived next door to him for so long, hiding how she felt, what she'd hoped for.

"What is it?" He tucked her hair behind her ear in that loving way he had.

"Did you know I had a crush on you?"

Shock splashed his expression. "No."

"Since the day I moved in. You had moved in the week before, remember?"

He didn't nod or shake his head, only stared at her.

She giggled nervously. "Say something."

"You wouldn't even look at me. I thought you didn't like me, only Carrot Cake." The little dog lifted his head at the mention of his name. He put his front paws on Emery's legs, and she lifted him into her lap.

"See?" Archer said. "You like him best."

"I like you best," she whispered, a long sigh following. "I need to find another job."

"We still have a month at the ranch."

"You'll get that job." She sat up and carefully dropped

Carrot Cake to the ground. "With Glenna here, I'll need something else."

"It'll be cheaper with her here, right? You won't be paying two electric bills."

"Probably."

"Why didn't she just live with you before?"

"She doesn't want to burden me." Emery rubbed her face and found it crusty. "But she did, even when she wasn't here." Her shoulders felt so heavy, it was almost impossible to believe. "My father abandoned us after her accident. My mom had to sell the farm, and we moved here. I won't do that to her."

"Em," he said, real soft. He rubbed her back. "You're a great person."

She shook her head. "I tried to steal your job. I still hope I'll get it and not you. I'm not that great of a person." She stood, grateful her legs had the strength to hold her upright. "I'm sure my mom's here by now. I should go."

"Emery." He stood too and caught her arm. "Can I come eat with you guys?"

She marveled at his forgiving nature. Half of her wanted to push him away so he wouldn't have to share her burden, and the other half desperately needed the support. She battled with herself, finally deciding that she simply wanted him by her side.

"Sure, of course," she said, feeling selfish and hoping he didn't mind taking some of her weight for a little while.

Emery secured her hand in Archer's before she opened the front door and re-entered her town-home. Her mom had indeed arrived, and she had a spread of white boxes from Pan's on the kitchen counter. The sharp scent of the orange sauce on their chicken met her nose and reminded her that she hadn't eaten in hours.

"Emersyn." Her mother hurried toward her and hugged her. Emery thought her mom felt skinnier than last time she'd seen her. She'd always been rail thin, and Emery had learned her bird-like eating habits from her mom, who was always grabbing an apple or a bag of nuts as she rushed from her job at the bookstore to her job at Migliano's, an upscale Italian restaurant. On Saturdays, she helped at the library for a few hours.

"Hey, Mom." Emery felt a similar level of acceptance and comfort from her mom, but she didn't want to come home to her mom. She wanted to come home to Archer. She stepped out of her mom's embrace. "This is my boyfriend, Archer Bailey."

Her mom scanned him from head to toe, her eyes stalling on the cowboy boots and then the hat. She smiled at him. "Hello, Archer."

He tipped his hat. "Ma'am."

"Oh, we're huggers." Her mom stepped into Archer, and she looked like a dwarf next to his tall frame and wide shoulders.

Archer chuckled and received her mom into a friendly hug, meeting Emery's eyes over her mom's head. They sparkled like fool's gold, and Emery grinned at him before sauntering over to the Chinese food.

"What do you want, Glenna?"

"I already took her something," Emery's mom said. "We ate, so go ahead and take what you want."

Archer joined her in the kitchen, stepping too close to be friendly and glancing down at her with a playful glint in his eye.

"Behave," she whispered. "My *mother* is here."

He growled, scooped orange chicken onto his plate, and winked at her before joining her family in the living room.

Emery took her time with the food, mostly because she needed a few extra minutes to sort through her feelings. The easy way Archer assimilated himself into the conversation, watching Glenna when she spoke, laughing at something her mom said.

She couldn't help feeling like she'd made the best and worst decision of her life to start dating him, and she wasn't sure what would happen when Christmas came and they couldn't ride up to the ranch together anymore.

———

Archer detected a change in Emery over the course of the next couple of weeks. He'd expected it, but he didn't know how to handle it. Didn't know what to say to her. Didn't know how to help her beyond carrying Glenna up the stairs in the evening and back down in the morning.

He and Emery still drove to work together every day, but their conversations weren't as robust, and she hadn't kissed him in that super passionate way in days.

He worked with another recruit, cleaning watering troughs in the barn, his thoughts far from making sure everything got sanitized and refilled for the horses. Archer still won the star over Clyde, further cementing his future victory.

He wasn't as happy about it as he thought he should be. His relationship with Emery had cast a cloud over the job at Horseshoe Home, and he found himself wondering if he should focus on one thing at a time.

Finally, the day before Thanksgiving, with the scent of pumpkin pie hanging in the air at the administration lodge, he found Emery in the kitchen, washing her hands. "Can I talk to you for a second?" he asked.

She glanced at him in surprise, her blonde braid resting on her shoulder. "Now?" They didn't normally converse much beyond saying hello or nodding while at work. Somehow, though, everyone at the ranch knew they were together.

"Yes, now." He nudged her toward the room at the back of the kitchen that used to be a mudroom when the building was used as a house. He closed the door behind them, sealing them in. "I need to know what you're thinking," he said.

"About what?"

"Everything." He blew out his breath. "You don't talk to me anymore."

Shutters flew over her eyes, and his frustration grew. "Nothing to say," she said, doing that thing she used to do where she wouldn't look directly at him.

"I know that's not true." He fisted his hands so he wouldn't twine his fingers with hers. "Em, what's going on?"

"What's going on?" The words exploded from her mouth. "What's going on, Archer, is that I've come to rely on you, and I hate that." She set her mouth into a tight line and shook her head.

"I like helping you."

"And it makes me feel weak. I'm not weak."

"I never said you were."

"I have work to do." She brushed past him and pulled open the door. Archer had no idea what was going on, or why him coming over to carry her sister up to her bedroom would make Emery feel weak. She still couldn't lift a single bale of hay by herself. Why did it matter if he helped out?

"What are you doin' in there?" Jace peered at him with confusion in his eyes. He held a sandwich in his hand.

"Emery said she doesn't like relying on me." Archer didn't know where the words had come from, or why he'd thought his personal problems should be laid at the feet of his boss. "I don't get it."

Understanding flowed into Jace's expression and he removed the sandwich from the bag. "She's a strong-willed woman, that one."

"Yeah." Archer sighed. One of the qualities he'd always admired about Emery was the one that would come between them? He didn't like that. "So what do I do?"

"Let her be her."

"She can't carry her sister up the stairs. Someone has to do it."

"Do they?" Jace shrugged. "Probably doesn't help that you're the superstar around here, earning more stars than even some of my veteran cowboys."

"I—" Archer didn't know what to say.

"You're a natural cowboy, Archer. We'd be lucky to have you here." Jace took a bite of his sandwich and chewed. He swallowed and said, "In fact, pretty much the only way I'm not going to hire you is if you quit." He ducked his cowboy hat and left the kitchen.

Archer's disbelief roared, and his spirit shot toward the sky. Jace had all but offered him the job, right there, right then. He stepped out of the mudroom, part of him rejoicing and the other part in a tailspin.

He'd wanted this job so badly he could taste it, had dreamt about it.

But he also wanted Emery, and he had the distinct feeling that he couldn't have both.

———

He spent Thanksgiving Day with his parents. Neither of his brothers came home, and the holiday passed with turkey and mashed potatoes, pecan pie and vanilla ice cream, and a short list of things Archer was thankful for.

Emery topped the list. So did Horseshoe Home Ranch and Jace and the fact that Archer now knew he could be a career cowboy. After all, a compliment from a ranch owner like Jace wasn't taken lightly.

The day after Thanksgiving, when Gold Valley shops were full of people buying Christmas gifts, he drove up to the ranch with Emery. There'd been something unspoken between them since he'd pulled her into the mudroom last week, and he hated it.

"Is this how we are now?" he asked as she turned Jenny onto the ranch road.

"I don't know."

"Do you want me to stop coming over to help with Glenna?"

"I don't know."

He *really* hated that she wouldn't look at him. "What can I do to make things better?"

"I don't know." She pulled into a space several paces down from the administration lodge, her shoulders boxy and tight. She opened her mouth to say something, thought better of it, and got out, leaving Archer alone with Jenny.

"I love you," he whispered to Emery's retreating form. "Don't you love me too?"

He knew what she'd say: *I don't know.*

Somehow he got through the day, earning three stars in the process of hauling hay and scrubbing out closets in the administration building. Apparently there was a lot more to ranching than just dealing with animals. He had to deal with men too.

"Hey," he said to Elliott near sunset. "Can you drive me home tonight?"

Elliott looked at him with questions in his eyes. "What?"

"Emery and I...I just need a ride home after work. If you can't, I'll ask Clyde."

"I can," Elliott said. "I need to get a few things at the grocery store anyway. Maybe a Christmas gift or two." He looked like he wanted to ask Archer more questions, but he didn't. He just went back to polishing the saddle he'd been working on.

Archer stepped outside and texted Emery. *Staying up here with Elliott. Don't need a ride home.*

She didn't respond, but by the time he made it back to the administration building, her car was gone. It felt like a silent breakup, and Elliott clapped his hand on Archer's shoulder. "I don't know what happened with you guys, but you seemed good together."

"We *are* good together." Archer stared down the empty lane, all the way until it turned and headed out to the main highway. "She—she's a strong-willed woman." He wouldn't talk badly about her, not to anyone.

He ate dinner with Elliott and even walked around the downtown shops and bought his mother a new teapot and his father a pair of leather work gloves. He knew Charlie liked puzzles and Xan enjoyed a good Rubik's cube, so he bought their gifts in the Hallmark store, which boasted games and stationery, cards and wrapping paper, figurines and keepsakes.

He didn't see anything for Emery, mostly because he didn't know what he might buy for her. He wanted to get her something, even if she was back to staring past him when they were forced into small talk in the backyard.

His heart rebelled at the idea that he wouldn't see her later that night, kiss her good-night after he carried her sister upstairs. But his brain knew he hadn't been kissing her good-night for a week now.

As Elliott dropped him off and he saw that all of Emery's windows were dark, a wild thought stole through his mind.

And he suddenly knew exactly what to give her for Christmas.

CHAPTER 10

$\mathcal{A}$rcher had never wanted Christmas to come so badly, not even when he was a child. He'd been driving up to the ranch by himself for two weeks, making plans with Jace, and Tom, and Ty, and Elliott for two weeks. Watching Emery's house and watching her at work for two weeks.

He didn't know what went on behind her closed doors, as he'd stopped going over there to help, something that ate at him until he called Doctor Pinnion, the pastor at church, and told him about Emery's sister needing help.

The very next morning, loud pounding on his front door had his heart racing. The adrenaline poured through him, igniting the competitive fire in his gut. Because he knew who stood on the other side, and that Emery would not be happy.

Sure enough, he opened the door to find lasers practically shooting from her eyes. "You called Doctor Pinnion about us?"

He casually draped his hand over the top of the door. "You need help. It can't be good for Glenna's back to sleep on the couch."

"You have no idea where she sleeps." Emery's fingers coiled into fists and she stalked off his porch and then back on it like a caged tiger.

"It was either Doctor Pinnion or Jace," Archer said calmly. "I figured you'd prefer help from the church than from the ranch."

Her face turned bright red, and Archer knew he'd made the right decision. "Of course, if you'd just let me come help Glenna…."

"Well, you're going to have to," she snapped. "She doesn't want some stranger carrying her up and down the stairs. Honestly, Archer."

"You wouldn't let me help," he said, his voice taking on a tone he didn't like. He schooled it back into submission. "Emery, all I've ever wanted to do is help you. It's why I've hauled your garbage can with all those silly bumper stickers out to the curb on Wednesdays, and why I happen to time my dog's potty breaks with when you're in the backyard." His chest hurt so much, so much.

"I've—I need—" Tears filled her eyes, but they weren't the same kind as last time she'd sobbed into his chest. That had come from grief, from fear, from pure exhaustion. These tears were angry, but Archer much preferred this animated version of Emery to the plastic doll she'd become since her sister had moved in.

"You need me." He reached out and took her hand. "I'm not going to abandon you when things get hard."

She yanked her hand away, her face turning pale. He'd never seen her so furious. "*Glenna* needs you to take her up and down the stairs." She spoke in a freaky calm voice that alerted Archer that he should probably back up before he got punched in the mouth.

Archer's hopes crashed and burned. He held onto the thought that he still had his Christmas present for Emery, but he realized he shouldn't have made any references to her father.

"I'll come by tonight," he said.

She shook her head, her tears spilling over. She wiped at them furiously. "No, this morning. She needs to shower."

"I'll be right over."

Emery nodded once and stomped away, leaving Archer with a hole in his chest where his heart should be. Still, he put on his boots and steeled himself to go next door. He knocked and waited, where he would've simply entered a few weeks ago.

"Come in," Glenna called, and Archer complied. The stench of an unwashed body hit him square in the face, but he put on a smile. Dishes littered the countertop in the kitchen, and the garbage obviously hadn't been emptied in weeks. Pure agony tore through him.

But he lifted Glenna as if she weighed nothing, as if she

smelled like a summer's rose, as if he hadn't been the cause of this disaster that sat only a wall away.

Christmas definitely couldn't come fast enough.

———

Emery strode along the sidewalks in the complex, estimating how long it would take Archer to get his shoes on and get Glenna up to the bathroom. She'd need to get home and help her sister into the shower before going to work. She checked her phone. Five more minutes.

She needed five more years to get over her pride and find a way through this blazing anger coursing through her. But Archer had had no right to call the pastor. No right whatsoever.

Just like you had no right to try to steal his job at the ranch.

The thought stopped her in her tracks. She hadn't thought about her behavior in a while, simply because Archer wasn't angry with her anymore. He'd forgiven her. He'd asked her what he could do to make things better between them, and she'd said she didn't know.

But she did.

There was nothing wrong with *them*. Only everything wrong with *her*. Glenna living with her made Emery's stress level atrocious, and she didn't sleep well, thinking every little sound was Glenna needing help.

She didn't want Archer to see this horrible, selfish side of herself, so she'd shut him out. There was a reason she hadn't had Glenna living with her, and it was all about

Emery. She didn't like the person she was when she was Glenna's caretaker, almost like Emery disappeared. She became a nameless, faceless servant, and she hated it.

In those moments, she understood perfectly why her father had left. She thought about leaving herself. And she absolutely could not face that side of herself, or allow anyone else to see it. Especially not Mr. Perfect, whose only problem came from disappointing his father five years ago.

Emery shook her head, her fury accelerating her pulse once more. Archer didn't understand, and she didn't want to explain it to him until he did. Eliminating him from her life was actually easier. At least she thought it would be.

But he was always there, ever present in her mind, lurking just across the fence and just around the corner at the ranch.

By the time she returned to her house, she was going to be late for work. She found she didn't care. She wasn't going to get the job at Horseshoe Home anyway. She entered through the backyard, sliding open the door that led into the kitchen.

She froze, the scent of powder and lilacs reaching her nose. The house had definitely not smelled like that when she'd left thirty minutes ago.

Every dish had been cleaned up. The dishwasher hummed underneath clean countertops. All the shoes had been put away, and the bags of trash she'd been piling by the door were gone. Glenna's blanket was nowhere to be found, nor any of her clothes and personal items. The entire bottom floor of Emery's townhouse looked like it was ready for a realtor to bring prospective buyers through.

She headed upstairs to find the washing machine running and Glenna waiting for her in the bathroom. "Hey." Emery leaned in the doorway. "Sorry I was gone for so long."

Glenna gave her a weak smile, the evidence of her tears plain to see on her cheeks. "He's a great man," she said. "I never tell you anything, Emery, except thank you. I know me being here is a huge burden for you. Don't you think I know that?"

Emery knelt in front of her sister. "Don't say that. I will always be here for you."

Glenna shook her head. "But you shouldn't be. You should be with Archer. Run away together, as far away as you can get."

Emery stared at her. "I could never—"

"But you *should*." Glenna's emphatic enunciation dove into Emery's eardrums, burrowing deep. Her sister took a long breath. "I don't know why you think you can't be with him. He doesn't understand either. Maybe you don't even know. But you should figure it out before you lose him. He's absolutely the best man for you, and you can't even see it."

Emery stood, her willingness to be lectured about Archer at a zero. "I'm going to be late, so let's get you in the shower."

She was, indeed, late. By almost an hour, and as soon as she walked into the administration lodge, Jace appeared at the end of the hall that led to his office. He waved for her to come on back, and her heart dropped to her heels.

"I'm sorry," she said when she entered the office. "My sister—"

"Archer told me." Jace held up his hand. "It's fine." He stared at her, and she could only handle the weight of it for a few seconds.

"I'm sorry," she said, dropping her gaze to her folded hands in her lap.

"You should be sayin' that to Archer, not me."

She raised her eyes back to Jace's, the familiar fiercely independent streak rearing its ugly head. "I don't think that's any of your business."

"When it affects my best cowboy, it's my business."

"Oh, so Golden Boy Archer is—"

"Archer is not my best cowboy." Jace folded his arms and nodded to someone over her shoulder. She turned, but not in time to see who'd been standing there.

Silence prevailed between them, while Jace frown-stared at her and she tried to riddle her way through the confusion infecting her mind. Ty entered the room, with Tom just behind him carrying the star chart.

"You're my best cow*girl*," Jace said. "And you were an hour late this morning. So it's my business what's going on with you."

Emery stared at the chart, where her stickers went right up to the top. She had so many, they'd started a second column for her. She shook her head. "This makes no sense. Those aren't—"

She realized then that hardly anyone else had any stars at all. Caleb, the cowboy who'd been winning, didn't have a single one. Neither did Elliott, who'd been in third place last time she'd checked.

And Archer's column was likewise empty. Her chest hitched and her tears came quickly. "I don't understand."

"Let's go outside," Tom said. "I think you'll get it then."

Emery had no idea what they were talking about, but she allowed them to corral her outside. She didn't have to look farther than the first cabin beside the administration lodge to find what they wanted her to see.

A man dressed as Santa Claus stood on the roof, holding a red bag that didn't seem to have anything in it.

"Emery," he called, and she knew it was Archer by the calming sound of his voice in her ears. Oh, how she wanted to hear that voice right before she fell asleep each night and first thing every morning.

"I love you, Emery Ender, and this Christmas, I'm standing up here on this housetop to give you what I hope will be the greatest gift of your life."

Tears streaked her face, and she couldn't look away from Archer, but she was aware that all the cowboys had gathered and were listening.

"Ask him what it is," Ty whispered. "He's got a script."

Emery glanced at the foreman. "A script?"

Ty grinned, also watching Archer. "Just ask him what the gift is."

She turned back to Archer dressed in that silly suit. A smile broke through her tears. "What's the gift?" she called.

The wind wanted to play in their game, because it whined as it tried to take off the hats of everyone present. Emery shivered without her coat.

"The stars," Archer called. "If I could lasso them down from the heavens for you, I would. But even I'm not that good." He grinned as the other cowboys chuckled. "But me and the boys here decided that you deserve as many stars as you can get. So we gave you some of ours."

He wasn't giving her the stars. He was giving her his job. She shook her head. "I can't let you do this." She knew how much this position meant to him, knew it was the start of a long career here at Horseshoe Home Ranch that he wanted desperately.

"No one denies Santa," he boomed. "Not while he's still up on the housetop."

She had no idea what to say. She glanced at Ty. "Now what?"

He shrugged, and Jace stepped forward. "He's waitin' for you to accept the stars."

"And you might want to do it quickly," Tom added. "I think Santa's starting to turn blue."

CHAPTER 11

Emery couldn't accept the stars. Not the stickers, and not the brilliant ones in the sky either. "I can't," she said to Jace. "Caleb deserves the bonus."

"He knew what he was giving up."

"Did his wife?"

"Of course," Jace said. "The ranch wives know pretty much everything."

Indecision plagued Emery. "I can't do this. Archer deserves the job."

"Archer wants *you*," Jace said. "Just say okay and then we can all get back to work. You guys can talk." He glanced at Tom, who wore a more sympathetic expression.

"He really would lasso the stars for you," Tom said. "He's got stars in his eyes when he talks about you. The man is dressed like Santa Claus, for heaven's sake." A smile accompanied the statement, then a chuckle.

Emery couldn't help her own laughter bubbling up her

"

chest either. She turned back to Archer, who possessed charm even in the red and white suit. He hadn't gone all the way and replaced his cowboy boots with Santa's black boots, though.

"A cowboy Santa, huh?" she called. "I guess I can't deny him."

Archer whooped—very un-Santa like—and headed for the edge of the roof. Elliott hurried from the crowd to hold the ladder, while Jace said, "It took him two weeks to get this set up, Emery. Be kind to him."

The men dispersed, seemingly in a moment, so that by the time Archer descended from the roof, Emery stood alone on the porch. She wrapped her arms around herself, a sense of apprehension in her stomach that didn't sit well.

Be kind to him.

Archer's boots tapped as he climbed the stairs. He wore a nervous look along with the festive costume.

"Where do you even get a suit like that?" she asked, trying for playful and achieving it pretty well, in her opinion.

"The North Pole, of course." He grinned at her, but the happiness that usually accompanied the gesture didn't reach his eyes.

"Sexy." She stepped closer to him and took a breath to get some of his cologne. Too bad it was so cold and her nostrils practically stuck together.

"Let's go inside," he said. "Santa is really cold."

"I didn't think Santa could get cold."

"Well, he can." He took her hand, the skin-to-skin contact making her heart beat erratically.

She let him lead her into the administration lodge and down the same hallway where Jace's office sat. Archer went past it and into a smaller room, which held a couple of chairs and a cot.

He sat, a sigh escaping his mouth. Not an exasperated sigh, but one full of weariness. Guilt that she'd caused that cascaded through her, but she sat too, determined to make things right between them.

———

"I'm sorry," Emery started. "I've messed up since the first day I met you." She hung her head, her ponytail falling over her shoulder and her cowgirl hat hiding her face.

Archer didn't need her apologies. "Em, I'm not mad about anything. When I first saw you up here interviewing, I was furious. I...I just couldn't lose another job to you. But I got over it."

"I can't take your job," she said.

"You're not. I'm giving it to you."

"I can't do it."

"Why not?"

She lifted her head and looked straight into his eyes. "I can't even lift a single bale of hay by myself. You're a born cowboy. This is what you were meant to do. And I'm going to take that from you?" She shook her head. "No. No way."

Archer took both of her hands in his. "So now what?"

"My distance from you had nothing to do with the job."

"But you need the job so Glenna can move out."

She sucked in a breath. "You knew it was about Glenna?"

"You completely changed when she came to live with you." Archer squeezed her fingers. "I may be just a cowboy, but I have eyes too."

"So you know this has nothing to do with you, right?"

"Oh, I think it has everything to do with me."

She cocked her head. "I—"

"You didn't want me to know that you resent her." Archer expected the fire that came into her eyes, and he got it. Red, hot fire. "But, Emery, I don't think any less of you because of how you feel about Glenna. It's a tough situation, and your fierce loyalty—one of the things I love most about you, by the way—won't let you simply wash your hands of her. I get it." He got it, because he couldn't just let his father's words die in his ears. Couldn't leave his father's opinion of him out of his decision-making.

She glared for a few more seconds before softening. "She's my sister. But I fear I'll be chained to her forever. I couldn't bind you to her too."

"What if I want to be bound to her?" Archer glanced at their entwined hands, his feelings so strong for Emery he didn't think they could be contained. "Because I'm in love with you Emery, and if she comes with you, I don't mind."

"I love you, too," she whispered, causing him to yank his gaze back to hers. He wondered for a nanosecond if he'd heard her correctly, but the shy smile she gave him testified that he had.

He leaned forward, almost off the edge of his seat, hoping she'd meet him halfway.

She did, and as she pressed her lips to his, Archer didn't think life could get any better. She giggled and ducked her head before the kiss turned too passionate.

"So now what, Santa?"

"Now we figure things out," he said. "It's what you and I have been doing our entire lives. We'll figure something out."

"One thing I know," she said. "You're taking this job. I'm not cut out to be a cowgirl."

"Oh, I beg to differ. You look great in those boots." He grinned and placed a gentle kiss on her cheek. "But I'll do whatever you say, Emery. I just want you to be happy. I want the woman back who told me stories about her childhood, and held my hand in the truck, and kissed me goodnight like she was my girlfriend."

Archer took a deep breath and forced himself to stop talking. He still really wanted this job, needed to be part of this ranch family. But he'd literally give anything to be with Emery, and that included this job.

"You earned the job, and I'm not taking it. I'll talk to Jace."

Archer couldn't help the smile that slipped across his face. "And what will you do for a job?"

She exhaled. "Oh, I don't know. I remember you saying something about waitressing or working at the grocery store." She gave him a wry smile and freed one of her hands to nudge his shoulder playfully. "Maybe Glenna and I can work at the same place. Maybe she can move in with my mother, or out on her own. I don't know."

"That piece doesn't have to be solved today. As long as we're okay today."

"I'm okay," she said in a voice that was barely audible. "I'm sorry about this morning."

"You know why I did it, right?"

"Yes, I know why you did it. But you didn't need to do my dishes or start my laundry."

Archer never wanted her to be in such a dark place that she completely stopped functioning. "I'll do whatever it takes to make sure every day is Christmas for you," he whispered. "Dishes, laundry, trash, or carrying your sister up the stairs."

"I don't deserve you." She traced her fingers down the side of his face, eliciting a shiver from him.

"You deserve the stars," he said before kissing her again, this time pouring every emotion he felt into the touch.

A knock on the door interrupted them this time, and Archer got up to answer it. Jace stood on the other side. "Announcement of winners is right around the corner," he said. "Can you tell me who won?"

"I won," Archer said as Emery looped her arm through his. "The job, the girl, all of it."

"So Caleb will get his bonus?"

"Yes," Emery said quickly. "I'll be fine."

Jace glanced at her. "I can have Belle ask around for jobs in the valley."

"That's not necessary," Emery said.

Archer stepped in front of her. "She'd love that. And her sister needs a job too. She's in a wheelchair, but she has cashier experience and can probably work in an office or something like that too."

"Archer."

He cut her a glance out of the bottom corner of his eye. "Emery." He ignored the tension against his arm. She needed to learn to accept help when it was offered, plain as that. "Anything you can find out, let us know."

"All right." Jace started down the hall, and Archer and Emery followed. He eased into the crowd and lingered near the back while Jace went to the front.

"Well, what an amazing four months it's been," he said. "We've gotten a lot of good things done, and I don't think anyone will be surprised to hear me say that Archer Bailey will be our new cowboy."

A cheer went up, and pride filled Archer's chest at the same time embarrassment heated his face. He took off his cowboy hat and waved it a few times, the way he'd seen rodeo champions do. He was about as far from a champion as a man could get, but he didn't want to seem arrogant or unappreciative.

"And the cowhands who earned bonuses this year are Caleb Chamberlain, Jerome Jackson, and Elliott Hawthorne."

"Aw, yeah!" Elliott pranced to the front of the room and accepted the envelope Jace extended to him. Archer laughed along with everyone else, tucking Emery against his side.

Immense gratitude filled him from top to bottom and front to back.

Thank you for putting me here, he prayed. *For Emery at my side. For Jace, and Elliott, and everyone here who's accepted me right into their family.*

Now all Archer had left to do was talk to his father.

———

"Dad!" he called later that evening. "Mom?"

"Archer." She rose from the dining room table. "What are you doing here?" She hugged him. "Is everything okay?"

"Fine, just fine." He couldn't stop smiling. "Where's Dad?"

"Oh, he's down in the basement, watching a documentary."

Archer grinned wider. "I love a good documentary."

"Two peas in a pod." His mom moved to the top of the stairs and called down to her husband. "Archer's here."

His dad came slowly up the steps, his eyes asking questions his voice didn't.

"I got the job, Dad." Archer embraced him when he reached the top of the stairs. "Jace Lovell said I was a natural-born cowboy." He laughed, relieved and satisfied when his father joined in.

"I knew you could do it," his dad said. "Good job, Archer."

"I'm gonna be a cowboy," Archer said, a note of awe in his tone. "Mom, I'm gonna be a cowboy!"

Archer pulled the cookie sheet out of his oven amidst a cloud of billowing, black smoke. He'd barely set the tray on the stovetop before the smoke alarm went off. Carrot Cake started yapping, like that would help at all.

"Dang it." He hurried over to the detector and started waving the oven mitt under it to clear the smoke and stop the beeping. The last thing he needed was the fire department over here. Or worse, Emery, wondering what he was doing.

Christmas Eve dinner required cookies in Archer's opinion, and he'd wanted to show up with the perfect chocolate chunk bites. Was that so wrong?

The shrill alarm finally stopped, and Archer turned back to the mess he'd made in the kitchen. Bowls and large utensils sat in the sink and covered the countertops. "This is why I make smoothies for breakfast and peanut butter sandwiches for dinner," he grumbled. Cooking and baking not only required some sort of culinary skill he didn't possess, but he also had to clean up afterward.

He took a deep breath and checked the recipe again. He still had dough left, and he scooped more balls onto a new cookie sheet. He slid it into the oven and double-checked the temperature. Three-fifty. He carefully set the timer this time, making sure he put in eight minutes and not eighty minutes. Maybe he'd get a dozen cookies to take next door. He just needed something to show Emery that he could do more than wrangle cattle.

His present for her sat near the front door, wrapped in sparkly red paper and a bright silver bow. Worry needled his mind; he hoped she'd like the new pair of cowgirl boots he'd found at the department store downtown. They had red stitching instead of pink, but they'd screamed Emery's name as soon as he'd laid eyes on them.

Beside them sat a long, rectangular package—a complete set of the Anne of Green Gables books—for Glenna. She'd told him once while he carried her upstairs that she loved the books almost as much as the movies. He'd gotten her both, hoping she didn't have them or hadn't brought them with her from Spokane.

The timer went off, and Archer pulled the cookies from the oven. They looked brown around the edges and he declared them a success with a grin and a "Finally."

At the appointed time, he gathered his cookies and his gifts and went next door.

Emery greeted him with a warm smile and a kiss. "You

made cookies?" She looked at them like they were hockey pucks and back at him with desire in her eyes. "You're a man of many mysteries." She grinned a flirty little grin. "I like that."

She took the cookies to the kitchen while he moved to put his presents under the tree. She'd decorated it with white lights, gold bows, and an assortment of white lace ornaments. A huge star adorned the top, and Archer gazed at it.

Emery returned and handed him a cup of hot chocolate. He put his arm around her, his soul singing. "This tree is beautiful," he said.

"Glenna makes the ornaments," she said. "Each one takes her about a month. She starches them into shape after she's crocheted them."

"Impressive." He looked to where Glenna sat on the couch, her ear buds in. She glanced at Archer and waved. He pointed to the ornaments and gave her the thumbs-up.

"I have two gifts for you tonight," Emery whispered. "One of them just isn't under the tree. I want to do it in private."

Archer very much liked the sound of that, and he pulled Emery a little closer. "I really would give you the stars, you know."

"I might ask you for them one day." Emery laid her cheek against his chest. "But for today, I'm just glad you showed up with cookies."

He chuckled and Emery signaled to her sister that it was time for dinner.

———

Emery kept one eye on Glenna and Archer as she added more milk to the mashed potatoes. They came together in a creamy consistency, and she added a dollop of butter and set the bowl on the counter. She had a tiny dining room table, so they'd serve themselves buffet-style and then sit down.

She pulled the ham and the roasted vegetables from the oven, where she'd been keeping them warm, and lined everything up. With the rolls on the end, she called, "Time to eat."

Archer pushed Glenna into the kitchen, his eyes alight with love and laughter. Emery loved him, and a warm glow, like a low light bulb, switched on in her core. Though she wasn't proud of what she'd done that had enabled her to spend these last four months with him, the result was wonderful.

They ate with candles on the table and the scent of Christmas pine in the air. Halfway through dinner, snow began falling beyond the sliding glass door. Carrot Cake went over to the glass and yapped, turning back to look at Emery as if to say, "Look! Snow!"

She giggled and went to the door, pressing one palm against the icy glass. She watched the flakes fall for a moment, absolute joy and wonder threading through her. She sighed as she bent to pick up Archer's dog and returned to the table.

He watched her with a knowing glint in his eye and

asked Glenna about her new job at the city offices. Emery listened to her talk about the work there, and how much she liked it.

"Emery drops me off every day," she said, glancing at Emery. "But I'm hoping I can move out in the spring. Gold Valley doesn't have as many services as Spokane, but if I can get an apartment downtown, I can just walk to work."

The warmth in Emery's chest expanded at the increased confidence and happiness she saw in Glenna. After all, all Emery had ever wanted for Glenna was for her to be happy.

"Let's do gifts." Archer practically leapt from the table and collected the presents from under the tree. He cleared dishes and replaced them with wrapped boxes, his entire person shining with radiance.

"You go first Glenna," he said.

She ripped the green paper from his box, revealing her favorite books and movies. "Archer." She squealed. "This is the best! Thank you so much."

He leaned over and kissed her forehead, and Emery's opinion of him skyrocketed. "Your turn," he said to her.

She carefully took off the silver bow and removed the sparkly red paper. A boot box sat inside, and her chest cinched. "Boots?"

"Just open the box." He folded his arms, an edge of anxiety in his eyes.

She lifted the lid and a beautiful pair of dark leather cowgirl boots sat inside, with red stitching in beautiful flower and horseshoe patterns. She inhaled sharply. "Oh, Archer, these are beautiful." And they'd probably cost a fortune, which made her want to refuse them. She worked to shove that impulse down. She wanted to accept things from him. His help. His gifts. His love.

"They have horseshoes on them," he said. "To represent the ranch where we fell in love."

She met his eye. "I didn't fall in love with you at the ranch."

"No?" His eyes held only amusement now.

She shook her head, wishing she could have her private moment with him right now. "No, I fell in love with you right here. Maybe in the backyard one day. Or maybe listening to your blender every morning. Or maybe in Jenny, on our way up the ranch."

He stood and came around the table to kiss her. "Well, I fell in love with you on the ranch, so I hope you like the boots."

"I love them." She pressed her forehead to his and cleared her throat. "Okay, my turn." She handed out her gifts, glad when Glenna liked the new blouses Emery had bought for her to wear to her new job.

Archer pulled the paper off his favorite candies—a giant bag of only red Starburst. He chuckled and ripped into the treats straightaway.

"There's more," she said, nodding to the package wrapped in blue snowmen. He opened the smaller package and pulled out a pocketknife she'd had engraved with his initials. "I thought maybe you could use it on the ranch," she said.

He beamed at her. "Thanks, sweetheart."

Their attention turned to Glenna, and her gifts, and finally Archer pushed her back into the living room where she picked up her book and started reading.

"We're gonna go for a walk," Emery said, wondering for the millionth time if that phrase bothered Glenna.

She barely glanced up from her romance novel and said, "All right."

Emery exchanged a glance with Archer before running upstairs to get the gift she'd reserved for when they could be alone. Her heart pounded in her chest so hard she could barely breathe past it.

The ring box seemed to weigh a thousand pounds, and she had no way to conceal it. She cursed herself for not grabbing her winter coat first. She cracked the lid, wondering if she could just tuck the ring in her pocket.

The overhead lights glinted off the white gold of her grandfather's ring. It wasn't a wedding band, but Emery had been practicing what she was going to say to accompany the gift. Inlaid rows of yellow gold glimmered, and her hope and confidence increased.

Archer had professed his love for her several times. He'd accept the ring. Still, a niggle of doubt tugged at her.

"Emery?" he called up the stairs.

She snapped the lid closed and palmed the ring box. After she'd hurried downstairs, he helped her into her coat, and she managed to pocket the box without him seeing. Outside, the frigid Montana air bit at her exposed skin. She wiggled her fingers into gloves and joined her hand with Archer's.

He sighed and said, "This has been a great year."

"Yeah?"

"Well, maybe not the first half. When I lost that job at Silver Creek to you…." He inhaled and exhaled, his breath hanging in front of them as they strolled. "But it got better. We didn't quit."

Soft light from the lamps along the sidewalk illuminated the snow. The bulbs closest to the clubhouse had been replaced with red and green bulbs, and the picturesque Christmas scene before her prompted Emery to pause.

"So I have another gift for you," she said, her recited lines coming easily to her mind. "It might be kind of strange, but it's not what you think, I swear." She pulled out the ring box and held it up. Archer simply stared at it.

"I love you," she said. "And this is my grandfather's ring. I never met him, but my mom says he was one of the hardest workers she ever knew. And he was kind, and faithful, and you sound so much like him that I wanted you to have it."

He took the box but didn't open it. "Are you proposing to me?"

"No." She giggled. "That's why I said this wasn't what you might think it was." She touched his fingers. "Open it."

He did, peering at the ring for a few seconds before he pulled it out. "It's really nice," he said. "How do I wear it?"

"It goes on the middle finger of your right hand." She removed the ring from the box while he slipped his right hand out of his glove. "It's not like a promise ring for men or anything. It's just a…."

"Family heirloom," he said. He stared at his hand as she

pushed the ring onto his finger. "A reminder of who to be, even when no one's watching."

When he looked at her again, his eyes shone like wet glass. "It's wonderful. Thank you." He gathered her into his arms and it felt like he was drawing her right into his heart. He touched his lips to hers and said, "I love you," before claiming her mouth and kissing her so completely it didn't matter if she never got another Christmas gift. She had Archer, and he was all she ever needed.

CHAPTER 13

*A*rcher much preferred summer ranching to winter ranching, but he would never admit it to Elliott. The two men had been sharing a cabin on the end of the row for six months, and with the arrival of June, Archer could sense and smell something in the air that hadn't been there through the long, cold months.

Hope.

A new beginning.

For the ranch, and for Archer personally.

He stepped back into the house with his empty coffee mug. After placing it in the sink, he collected the navy blue ring box from its treasured position on top of the microwave. It had been sitting there for three months, empty, while Archer saved enough money to buy Emery a wedding ring.

He was making the trip down to the jeweler today.

Today. A smile graced his face, and he tried unsuccessfully to wipe it away as Elliott entered the kitchen.

"What are you smilin' about?"

"We got paid today."

"Yeah, so?"

"I'm gonna go buy Emery her ring."

Elliott didn't react as he retrieved his coffee mug from the dish drainer and poured himself a cup. Archer always woke before Elliott, always made the coffee, always got them out the door on time. It was a miracle Elliott had been able to function in the mornings before Archer came along.

"Want me to come?" Elliott spooned sugar into his coffee and faced Archer.

"Yes." A twinge of guilt accompanied the word. Elliott was five years older than Archer and not currently dating anyone. He'd confessed to Archer that he hadn't much luck with the ladies, and Archer knew seeing Emery and Archer together was hard on him.

"I bet Em can set you up with someone," he said. "Now that she's working at the elementary school."

Elliott nodded. "I'm sure she can."

"Want me to ask her?"

Elliott had always declined when Archer had talked to him about such things in the past. Today he said, "Why not?"

Archer grinned. "C'mon, we're gonna be late."

Elliott downed his coffee and set the mug in the sink. "How are you going to ask Emery to marry you?"

"I don't know," Archer said. "Do you have any ideas?"

"I can't even get a date. How would I have any ideas for

how to ask a woman to marry me?" He gave Archer a sour look. "Plus, I don't want to get another roommate. I secretly pray that you two will break up."

Archer tipped his head back and laughed. He knew Elliott had done no such thing, but Archer did send a silent prayer heavenward that Elliott could find someone to share his life with who didn't already work at the ranch.

That evening, Archer stared blankly at the jewelry cases. "Maybe I should've brought Emery," he said. "What if she hates what I pick out?"

The salesman offered no support, and Elliott barely glanced up from his phone. "She'll like what you get," he said. "It's a diamond."

"And they're expensive." Archer studied the case again. "Let me see that one again." He pointed in the general direction of a yellowish diamond he'd already looked at. "What did you call it again?"

"A cape diamond," the salesman explained. "They're mined off the cape of South Africa, and they're in the yellow diamond family. One of the lightest ones." He removed the diamond and handed it to Archer. He liked the shape of the stone, the beautiful way it resembled a star in both color and appearance.

"We have a fancy light yellow diamond over here." The salesman moved down several feet. "You can see this one has a richer yellow coloration." He took out a ring that had a diamond shaped stone in a deeper yellow than the one Archer held. "And it's a marquise shape."

He liked the color better, but the diamond itself was an

odd shape. He wondered if Emery would like it better than the more square one he held. "What shape is this?" he asked.

"That one's princess cut," the salesman said.

Princess, Archer thought. That seemed to fit. "I like this one best."

"And you wanted the engagement piece too?"

He swallowed and reminded himself that he'd been saving for six months in order to buy this ring. "Yes," he said.

"Do you know the size?"

Archer's mind blanked. He had no idea there'd be so many variables in a ring. Shape, size, setting, color, even the type of band had taken him fifteen minutes to decide. "What's a normal size?" he asked.

"We can do a seven," the salesman said. "If she needs it resized, she can bring it in and we'll do it for free."

Archer nodded and handed over the princess cut cape diamond. He hoped he'd gotten all those words in the right order.

"We'll size it and clean it," the man said. "Give us about thirty minutes."

Suddenly anxious to be out of there, Archer approached Elliott from the watch cases and said, "They need thirty minutes. Want to grab a waffle?"

"That's the only reason I came with." Elliott grinned at him and they left the jewelry shop in favor of downtown Gold Valley, where a Belgian waffle shop had come to town a couple of years ago. They served amazing combinations of authentic Belgian waffles, with fruit, nuts, and chocolate.

They even made sandwiches out of their waffles, though Archer hadn't tried one of those yet.

And he didn't tonight either, but ordered his favorite Belgian waffle—the apple pie waffle. With caramelized apples, whipped cream, and a cinnamon-infused waffle, he was in heaven with only one bite.

"Do you think I could just stop by her house and ask her?" he asked.

"Seems kind of boring." Elliott cut off a piece of his chocolate stuffed waffle and delicious Belgian chocolate oozed onto the plate. "I mean, you stood on the roof in a Santa suit to get her back. Seems like that's the bar."

Archer frowned and swallowed his bite of apples. "Seems like a high bar I'll never be able to reach again." Worry riddled him. Was that really the bar? Did Emery really expect him to do something that elaborate with everything he did?

He shook his head. She wasn't like that, though he did suspect he needed to do more than simply stop by her townhome and drop to one knee. She worked at the elementary school only a few blocks from where he sat.

"What about if I...go to the school and call her down to the office? Propose there?"

"Maybe," Elliott said.

"The waterfalls? She likes them, and we've started going there after work now that it's summer."

"Sure."

With his friend completely disinterested in adding to the conversation, Archer let it drop. But ideas—all bad, in his opinion—continued to rotate through his mind. He couldn't settle on one, so he simply went back to the jeweler and collected the ring. The box went right back on top of the microwave, almost mocking him.

He just needed a plan for his proposal.

———

Emery loved her new job. She had never pegged herself for someone who liked to work with kids, but she did enjoy the time she got to spend with the students out on the playground. She monitored three recesses a day—one in the morning, one at lunch, and one in the afternoon. When she wasn't doing that, she made copies and booklets for the teachers.

The work was easy, the building was air conditioned in the warm months and heated in the cool months, and she got to wear cute shoes to work. She'd even made several friends.

Glenna had moved out at the end of April, leaving Emery to herself for the past month. She loved the quietness of her house when she came home and when she woke. She missed having Archer right next door, but she went up to the ranch a few times a week, or they met for dinner or at the waterfalls, or he came to her house.

She dreamed of the day they'd be married and be able to stay up all night, whispering in the dark, and then wake tangled in each other's arms. But Archer hadn't brought up marriage once, and Emery certainly wasn't going to.

He lived at Horseshoe Home now, and she wondered if there was even a place for her there. She knew some of the cowboys had a private cabin for them and their families, but those men seemed to be veterans, men who'd worked at Horseshoe Home longer than six months, men with important ranch positions.

She stapled a note to a form and set it in the pile. Pick up papers, match corners, staple. She repeated the action over and over, the radio in the corner playing a song she could barely hear. Plenty of time and energy for her mind to wander in circles around her future.

School would be out next week, and she didn't get paid when she didn't work. So for the next two months, she wouldn't have any income. She'd already lined up a part-time job at the recreational center as a custodian.

Whatever she had to do, she did it.

Maybe you should propose to Archer, she thought. But she remembered his wary look at Christmastime, and she decided she could be patient for just a little while longer.

That afternoon, after work but before Archer was set to arrive, she slipped into her swimming suit and went to the pool in her townhome development. She loved the sun, though the snow held wonder for her too, and she enjoyed a couple of lazy hours with just her, a pair of sunglasses, and music lilting through her headphones.

Her phone buzzed on her stomach, and she lifted it to see the screen. *I'm here. Where are you?*

Emery smiled. *At the pool. I'll walk back.* She stood and gathered her towel and sunscreen, dumping them both in her pool bag. Sure enough, when she unlatched the back gate, she caught a glimpse of Archer through the sliding glass door.

He looked tense and he paced from one corner of her kitchen counter to the front door and back. She entered and said, "Hey. What's going on?"

"I think I left something of mine in Jenny, and she's locked." His nervous energy filled the whole bottom floor, and she hoped whatever he needed wasn't too important.

"Oh, well, let me get the keys."

His phone rang and he said, "It's Jace. Can you go check for me?" He lifted his phone to his ear and said, "Hey, Jace," before she could even ask what she should be looking for.

Confused, and slightly irritated, she went out to the driveway where she'd left Jenny, who also liked a bit of sunshine in the summertime. She hadn't seen anything in Jenny over the past couple of weeks, and she had no idea when he'd left the mystery item.

She opened the passenger door—which wasn't locked— where Archer always sat when she drove. A navy blue ring box stared back at her.

In slow motion, like someone had encased her whole body in slow-drying plaster, she reached for the box. Heat burned her fingers when she touched it, and she jumped when Archer said, "You found it."

In one swift motion, he took the box from her, cracked the lid, and dropped to one knee. "I know this isn't the most romantic gesture," he said. "But you said you fell in love with me right here, or maybe in the backyard, or maybe in

Jenny. So I thought she could be trusted to hold the ring until I could give it to you."

Emery pressed both hands to her chest as she volleyed her gaze from Archer's hope-filled face to the beautiful diamond in the box. "Archer." Her voice shook.

"I love you, Emery. Will you be my wife?"

"Yes!" She shook as she extended her left hand and he slid the ring onto her finger. He took her in his arms and kissed her, sending explosions of heat and happiness through every corner of her body. She'd need another dip in the pool to cool down after that kiss, but she didn't mind. She didn't mind one little bit.

Because she was kissing her fiancé.

CHAPTER 14

Emery couldn't believe she was trying to pull off a wedding in only three months. But when she'd mentioned April, Archer had nearly come apart, claiming he didn't want to wait one more day to make her his wife.

She didn't want to wait either. Sending him back up the canyon at midnight was hard enough. So she'd re-evaluated, and they'd decided they should get married over Labor Day weekend, almost exactly one year to the day when they started spending more time together as friends instead of just acting like acquaintances who shared a wall.

And since Emery wasn't working nearly as much, she'd poured her time and energy into planning the best wedding she could on a tight budget. She made all the centerpieces out of silk flowers she bought at the craft store on clearance. She was only using fresh flowers for her bouquet and Archer's boutonniere.

She'd found a simple white dress at the boutique downtown and her mother had been sewing lace and jewels onto it for the past two months. She'd reserved the clubhouse in her townhome development for the reception, and she'd bypassed hosting a dinner completely, which made her largest expense paying to use the church for the actual marriage ceremony.

Archer had offered to ask Jace if they could use the ranch, but Emery had never envisioned herself getting married with more animals than people in attendance. She'd never actually envisioned herself getting married, but now that she was, she wanted it to be in a church.

She'd had Belle take their engagement pictures and design an announcement, and the postage and envelopes were a close second for a major expense. Emery had budgeted down to the penny, and she was happy that she was coming in right at her fifteen-hundred-dollar limit.

She admired the wedding dress hanging on her bedroom door. Her entire counter downstairs was covered with the floral arrangements, and her fridge and freezer were packed with cookies and milk—Archer's only contribution to the planning. He'd wanted a cookie and milk bar for the reception, and she'd agreed because both of those items were easy to make and cheap to buy.

None of it mattered anyway. As long as they showed up at the church and got married in the morning, would anyone really care what they ate at the reception, or what her dress had looked like, or if the roses on the tables were real?

Emery didn't think so, and she woke the next morning

with a smile on her face. Her mother arrived with Glenna just as she was stepping out of the shower, so Emery hurried to dress in her sweats so Glenna could do her hair and makeup before her mother would drive them all over to the church.

They chatted while Glenna brushed and curled and pinned. Their mother gushed over the "elegant up-do" and then Glenna started on Emery's makeup. "Remember, I want to be a little natural," she said.

"I haven't forgotten," Glenna said. She worked her magic with brushes and pots of color until she finally said, "You are beautiful," in a voice choked with emotion.

Emery opened her eyes, which felt a little heavier than she was used to, and went into the half bath to look at herself. A true beauty stared back, a smile forming on her face. Her mother joined her, squeezing her shoulders as she said, "I'm so happy for you."

Emery blinked back the tears, not wanting to ruin the makeup job her sister had meticulously performed. She returned to the living room and hugged Glenna. "You should be a makeup artist," she said.

"Really?" Hope entered Glenna's eyes, and Emery determined to look into what it would take for Glenna to truly become a makeup artist.

"Really." Emery sighed. "Now, we better get over to the church so we don't run into Archer." She collected her shoes and dress while her mom helped Glenna out to the car. They arrived at the church and headed inside to the bride's room, where she slipped out of her sweats and into her slip.

Her mom helped her into the lacy dress and found an errant edge that needed to be sewn. She whipped out her trusty sewing kit and fixed the lace so it laid right. "There. Now, let's get the traditional items."

Emery hadn't cared about having something borrowed, or something blue, but her mother really wanted her to observe the old English rhyme. "So for something old, I brought my grandmother's ring." She produced a gold ring on a chain. "It's mine, and I'm not quite ready to let it go yet, so it's going to count for something borrowed too."

She looped the chain around the handle of the bouquet, which she lifted out of the vase of water it sat in. She used a pearly pin to secure it in place amidst the flowers. "There. That something old gives you continuity," she said. "And heaven knows you need that. We all do." She smiled lovingly at Emery, who couldn't help smiling back.

"The something borrowed gives you borrowed happiness until you're able to give it to someone else." She reached up and brushed her fingers across Emery's bare shoulders. "But you've always been the one to give happiness to me and Glenna, so it's our turn today."

She turned back to Glenna. "You brought the something new?"

Her sister reached into the mesh bag that hung on the right side of her wheelchair. "Right here, Mom." She passed their mother something Emery couldn't see.

"Something new," her mom said. "Offers you optimism for the future. You and Archer deserve so much for your future, and I hope you'll have it." She presented a charm in the shape of a cowboy boot. "So Glenna and I got you this. After the wedding, you can put it on the chain and wear it as a necklace. You can put it on a bracelet too."

"Mom." Emery's voice cracked. "Thank you. You too, Glenna." She took the charm and studied it. Her future did belong with a cowboy, and the boot was a perfect representation of that. Her mom took the charm back and attached it to the chain.

"And for something blue, we put in those two blue hydrangeas in your bouquet." She grinned down at the beautiful flowers, which also included white roses and deep plum carnations. "The something blue stands for purity, love, and fidelity." Her mom glanced up. "We wish you and Archer every happiness life has to offer."

Emery hugged her mom and then her sister. Someone knocked on the door, her cue that it was time to get going. Her father wasn't there to walk her down the aisle, and a twinge of sadness radiated through her.

She hadn't spent any time missing the man who had walked out on her. She didn't know where he was, and she wasn't sure she would've invited him had she known. What she did know was that her sister was going to go down the aisle first, blowing bubbles, and her mother was going to escort Emery to Archer's side.

They proceeded out of the bride's room, and the chatter in the chapel ceased when the wedding march began. Emery took a deep breath as Glenna made the first turn of her wheels.

"You ready?" her mom whispered.

"So ready," Emery said back, the vision of Archer down at the end of the aisle so exciting her skin started humming. She waited until Glenna had passed several rows before Emery took her first step.

The aisle seemed much longer now than any other time she'd been in this church. The weight of everyone watching her—from old friends from other jobs, to her new friends at the elementary school, to every single cowboy from Horseshoe Home Ranch—made her nervous and sweaty.

But when her mother passed her to Archer, everyone disappeared. It had always only been him, even before Emery had realized he was right there, living next door. She grinned up at him, ready to become his wife.

Archer could barely stand. His nerves and excitement blended together until he couldn't tell if he was a happy excited or about to throw up. The weight of Emery's hand on his arm indicated she was experiencing similar nerves.

He leaned down and whispered, "You're beautiful," just as Doctor Pinnion started the ceremony. The pastor had a deep voice that reached right into Archer's chest and struck chords. He always said good things on Sunday, and today he spoke about love and friendship and how they went hand-in-hand.

Archer felt very lucky to be marrying his best friend. Though they couldn't afford to go on a huge honeymoon, he had arranged a three-day weekend up at a cabin on Bear

Mountain. Well, Jace had arranged it with a former employee of the ranch who'd moved to Utah and bought a horse ranch. Apparently, Landon owned a cabin and he was more than willing to let Archer and Emery use it for the weekend.

Emery didn't know about that yet, and Archer's enthusiasm nearly burst into the pastor's beautiful speech. He finished and looked at Archer and Emery. "Well, I don't think I've ever seen such a fine couple. Are you ready to get married?"

"Yes, sir," Archer said at the same time Emery nodded.

"I suppose that's why we're all here." The pastor grinned out at the crowd, the gesture infectious. "So, Emersyn Diane Ender, do you give yourself to this man, Archer David Bailey, to be his lawfully wedded wife, for your time on this earth, until death do you part?"

Archer looked at her, the moment of truth staring him in the face. She blinked up at him with those beautiful eyes. A few seconds passed.

"Em—" he started.

"Yes," she said. A rush of air left his lungs as she giggled. The pastor asked him if he'd take Emery to be his, and Archer said, "Yes," also.

"Kiss your bride, Archer."

A grin the size of Texas stretched Archer's face. He tipped Emery back and kissed her like he'd never kissed her before. She laughed and pushed on his chest as the crowd chuckled too.

He eased her back upright and took his cowboy hat off.

He placed it between them and the rows of people watching as he pressed his forehead to hers. "Finally," he said, right before kissing her properly.

Several of the cowboys whistled, but Archer didn't care, because he was finally kissing his wife.

"I have a surprise for you," he said, mashing his hat back on his head. "I hope you like the mountains."

She blinked at him before turning to the crowd and smiling. He led her back down the aisle and out of the building, where Jenny waited.

Cheers and talking accompanied them as he helped Emery into the passenger seat and went around to get behind the wheel. He put a couple of blocks between them and the church before he told her about the cabin on Bear Mountain.

He turned toward the falls and the canyon. "We're going now?" she asked. "I'm not even packed."

"We have to come back for the reception tonight." He glanced at her. "Don't worry. I'll have you back in plenty of time to pack and get ready for that."

"What are we going to do between now and then?"

He reached for her hand and brought her wrist to her lips. "I have a few ideas."

———

Keep reading for a sneak peek at **LOVE AT FIRST COWBOY**, the final book in the Horseshoe Home Ranch Romance series.

Elliott Hawthorne opened the cabin door to a blast of air conditioning—thankfully—and the sight of Archer taping the top of a box. Unthankfully.

"Hey." He sighed and straightened his back with a groan. "You're still helping me move tonight, right?"

Elliott didn't want to, but as he closed the door behind him so he wouldn't air condition the ranch with all its September heat, he said, "Yeah."

"Don't sound so happy about it."

"I'm not happy about it." Elliott tried to smile to soften the words. "And I'm totally jealous you're going up to Landon's cabin on Bear Mountain."

Archer smiled, reminding Elliott why they'd gotten along so well as roommates. "So it's nice?"

Elliott also reminded himself that they would still be friends. Co-workers too. So Archer was getting married. Big deal. It was what adults did.

Well, everyone except for Elliott at least.

"It's really nice," Elliott said. "It's small, but intimate, and quiet, and it's a great place to relax and unwind." He wished he could go right now. Take his bay horse Precious with him and go. Skip Archer moving out. Skip Archer and Emery's wedding. Skip the whole Labor Day picnic—which he would attend alone. Again.

But the ranch was buzzing with all of the above. The cowboys didn't get off the ranch much in the late summer and early fall because of the harvest, but Ty, the foreman, had announced last week that minimal chores would be done on Labor Day and no one was allowed to come back until evening.

Elliott was planning to attend the picnic with the cowboys, and then he'd probably go visit his parents. He didn't get down to see them much because of his workload, but they were starting to get older and he knew he needed to make more of an effort to help them.

With two of his brothers already living in other cities, and one preparing to sell his carpet cleaning company and relocate, Elliott would be the only son left in Gold Valley soon enough.

"Need some help?" he asked as he unwrapped a granola bar. He didn't like to eat a lot for lunch, especially when it was really hot outside.

"I think I'm good," Archer said. "I moved up here with just two truckloads, so it shouldn't take long."

"You're buying me dinner after, right?" Elliott grinned at him.

Archer rolled his eyes. "Steak, if I remember your conditions."

"Hey, I have to drive you to the church tomorrow too," he said, scowling. "I deserve steak."

Archer's expression turned sympathetic, and Elliott hated it. He appreciated it too, but he really didn't need Archer's pity.

"So Andra didn't work out." He wasn't really asking.

"She…wasn't my type." Elliott was starting to think he didn't have a type. That no matter how many women he went out with, none of them would ever be a fit for him.

He'd had some luck with women in his early twenties, but the last five years had been a painful stretch of being single punctuated with first date after disastrous first date.

"Emery can check around better this time," Archer said, but Elliott shook his head and took off his black cowboy hat.

"I'm not interested in getting set up again," he said. "No more blind dates, no more friend-of-a-friend, none of it." Elliott's brown hair flopped around and he picked up his phone to text his barber. Maybe he could squeeze in a haircut between moving and the steak.

With the appointment set and his granola bar gone, Elliott left Archer to finish the packing and went back out to the ranch.

That evening, it took Elliott and Archer thirty minutes to load the boxes, clothes, and Archer's bed into two pickup trucks. "See you down there," Archer said, climbing behind the wheel of his smaller truck.

Elliott lifted his hand and got into his ranch truck to follow Archer to Emery's townhome. Another thirty minutes passed during the drive. Another thirty to get everything unloaded. Another thirty for the haircut.

Elliott was starting to wonder if he could just continue in this pattern. Thirty minute increments where he didn't have to worry about being single, where no one asked him who he was dating, where he didn't have to concern himself with meeting someone.

It sounded like a good plan, and he immediately adopted it.

Another thirty minutes later, he had his prime rib in front of him, a beautiful mid-rare cook on the meat and a pile of garlic mashed potatoes that made his mouth water. He ate the green beans and baby carrots because his mother had trained him to eat his vegetables and he'd trained himself to get that part over with first.

Archer asked questions about the cabin, and they talked about the ranch, and Elliott, drowsy on steak and potatoes, decided that it wasn't so bad that he'd be getting a new roommate in a couple of weeks. That he'd have to live alone until then.

Thank you for allowing me to be happy for him, Elliott thought as Archer set his credit card on the bill.

His phone rang, and Elliott checked the screen. "It's my brother," he said to Archer. "I'll meet you outside." He stood and swiped open the call. "Hey, Joel."

"Elliott."

With that one word, Elliott's insides iced. The food he'd eaten—which was a lot—solidified into cement.

"What's wrong?"

"Mom just called. Dad's fallen down and they're on their way to the hospital."

"Fell down? Where? How long ago?" He frantically patted his pockets to find his keys. Archer had planned to leave his truck at Emery's and ride back up the canyon with Elliott, but new arrangements would have to be made.

"About half an hour ago, and he was going to do some work in the backyard."

Guilt pulled through Elliott with the force of gravity. His father shouldn't be doing yard work; Elliott should've been going down and helping his parents out, the way Ty had been for the past few years.

"I'm on my way," he told Joel, turning back to talk to Archer.

One thirty-minute increment later, Elliott finally found his brother in the emergency waiting room. They embraced, and Elliott didn't like the worry in his brother's brown eyes. "Broken hip," Joel said. "He's going into surgery within the hour."

Two increments, Elliott thought. He could wait that long. Wait and worry, which was exactly what he did. His mother —his petite, sandy-haired mother—came through the doors only fifty-two minutes later. She'd been crying, and Elliott swamped her in a tight hug, his own emotions threatening to overflow.

"He's okay," she said as they all sat down in the waiting

area. "There's no reason for you boys to wait here. It's getting late. Go on home and get some rest."

Neither Joel nor Elliott moved. They exchanged a glance, and Joel leaned forward. "Ma, why don't you let Elliott take you home? He'll stay with you and I'll wait here to talk to the doctors when they come out of surgery."

Mom started shaking her head before Joel could even finish speaking, and Elliott knew she'd never leave Dad here.

Joel tried again anyway. "Mom, he'll be in there for a few hours. Elliott will bring you back when they finish."

Elliott put his hand on his mother's. "Ma, come on." To his surprise, she rose to her feet and went with him. Elliott tossed a look over his shoulder to his older brother, who nodded with a sad smile.

———

A week later, Elliott woke in the cabin by himself. He made a pot of coffee for himself, something Archer had been doing for nine months. He wasn't a morning person, so he'd let Archer set the alarms, make the coffee, and get them out the door. But he had to do all that himself now.

He'd been down to the valley every evening since his father's fall. His dad had been released from the hospital yesterday, and Joel had called late last night to ask Elliott to come down again tonight to meet the nursing staff that would be assisting their father for the next several months.

"I can't be there after the end of the month," Joel said. "I need you to handle it."

Elliott didn't want to handle it. He was the youngest of the four boys, and the only one not married. He worked twelve hours a day, and adding the care of his parents to his plate felt like it was going to choke him.

But he made it through the twelve hours and down the canyon to his parents' house. Joel's car was already there, as were two other vehicles, leaving Elliott to park on the street.

Get through this one increment, he coached himself before he entered the house, the familiar smell of marinara meeting his nose. His mother had likely been cooking all day, adding her tears into the homemade sauce while she waited for evening and her sons to come.

"Elliott," his mom said, coming down the hall from the great room where he assumed everyone would be. She drew him into a tight hug. "We're just fine," she whispered.

He drew back, confused. "Who says you aren't?"

"Elliott's here," Joel said before she could answer, and he joined them, drawing Mom back into the great room. Elliott followed, unsure of what he'd find once he rounded the corner.

The kitchen stretched to his right, with a dining set in front of a pair of French doors that led into the backyard. Four steps went down—the site of his father's fall.

A big living room filled the rest of space, with a large sectional that held Joel's wife and two kids on the longest side and two women on the shorter one.

Elliott's gaze landed on a woman with silver-purple hair that only reached her chin. It was very straight, not a hair out of place. She turned toward him, and everything around him fell away.

Only her brown eyes existed. Her heart-shaped face. Her timid yet strong smile.

Elliott needed to know her name, right now. Find out how she got her hair to fall like that. Her skin reminded him of the shimmery-white way the horizon shone when the sun was at its pinnacle, and he wanted to touch her, stat.

Everything rushed forward again, and Elliott managed to smile when Joel introduced the dark-haired woman next to the exotic beauty who'd rendered him breathless with a single look.

"And this is Holland Marsh," Joel said. "She's a physical therapist from the home health center."

Holland Marsh. Even her name was sexy, and Elliott reached out to shake her hand.

"Nice to meet you," she said, painting his world in glorious colors just with her voice.

His heart pounded, nearly romping around in his chest like a bull gone rogue. He felt ridiculous—or like he'd been transported back in time fifteen years, when he was ruled by first impressions and strong hormones.

"Hey, Dad," he managed to say, bending down to give his father a quick, soft hug. "I see Ma's made her spaghetti and meatballs."

His father smiled though Elliott knew he was in a lot of pain, and said, "You know how she is."

Elliott did, and he cut a quick glance at the violet-haired Holland, who wore a patient and kind smile for his dad. "She likes to cook for a crowd."

"Elliott," Joel said. "Since Demmie and I are moving to Sacramento, you'll need to sign the power of attorney papers."

Elliott tore his gaze from Holland, wrenched his mind away from his fully formed fantasies. "I'm sorry," he said. "Power of attorney?" He glanced at his mother, who stood with her arms cinched across her chest, everything making sense now.

Joel also watched their mom for a moment before turning back to Elliott with a long, impatient sigh. "They need help."

"With the yard," Elliott said. "The snow. The weeds." He normally didn't argue with anyone, but something told him this was wrong. "Joel, they're mentally sound. Dad just broke his hip. He didn't hit his head."

"I'm fine," Dad said, his voice barely audible.

"We're fine," Mom added, giving Elliott all the fuel he needed to see this through to the end.

"You go on to Sacramento," Elliott said. "I'll take care of Mom and Dad."

Joel looked like he wanted to argue. Instead, he stepped past Elliott and perched on the arm of the couch by his wife, Demmie. "Holland?" he asked.

"Your father needs a lot of care," the beautiful woman said, making Elliott's pulse zing through him like someone had hooked him up to a huge battery.

"I'm here," Mom said. "Elliott will come down from the ranch in the evenings. And you ladies will be here."

"Just one nurse, ma'am." Holland looked apologetic as she said it, her eyes filled with tenderness. "Your insurance only covers *one* home health nurse."

"We'll be fine," Mom said again, this time with a note of pleading in her tone.

Elliott met Holland's eyes, but she didn't give him an indication of what he should do. He did want the best medical care for his father.

"How about we just see how they do?" Elliott asked, swinging his gaze from his mother, to Holland, and to Joel. "Give them a couple of months and see how things go."

He looked hopefully back to Holland, as if she alone had the power to make this decision. Or maybe he just wanted to absorb the beauty of her face again.

She clasped her hands and gave him a small smile before ducking her head toward the other woman. "We'll leave you. See you tomorrow, Mister Hawthorne," she said to his father. She moved toward the corner, and Elliott's heart screamed at him to *go with her! Follow her! Get her phone number!*

"I'll be right back," he said to the room and went with them. "Excuse me?" he asked, causing both women to turn back.

"How often will you come?" he asked.

"The nurse will come a few times a week," Holland explained. "The physical therapist comes as often as the insurance will let me. In the beginning, that will be every day."

"What time?" He hoped he wasn't being too obvious, but he also really needed to know.

"Your brother has everything to explain the physical therapy," Holland said, not unkindly. In fact, she seemed good, and kind, and caring. She seemed strong, and capable, and sure of herself. Elliott wondered if that was his type. He sure hoped so.

"One more question," he said as she opened the door. "*You'll* be coming to do the physical therapy?"

A smile formed fully on her face, and Elliott almost got knocked backward from the brilliance of it. "No one has been assigned yet," she said. "We meet in the morning."

Elliott's heart plummeted, but he kept his face placid. "Okay, thanks," he said, his mind racing. At least he had one night to beg God to assign Holland to his father's care.

SNEAK PEEK! LOVE AT FIRST COWBOY CHAPTER TWO

*H*olland Marsh thought about the handsome cowboy that had blown into the Hawthorne house as she drove home. She didn't know anything about him, but something in his happy-hazel eyes had ignited something in her soul that had died when she'd left Idaho Falls.

Before that, actually. She'd simply decided to do something about the dead feelings inside, and that had prompted the move from everything she'd known in Idaho to Gold Valley, Montana, where her aunt and uncle had lived for thirty years.

Uncle Wallace had tried to get her a job at the equine rehabilitation center where he was the director, but she didn't have the right letters behind her name. Didn't matter. She'd gotten a job at a home health center easily enough. Seemed Montana had a shortage of physical therapists just like most other places.

She pulled into her cousin's driveway, her mind lingering on the black cowboy hat Elliott Hawthorne had been wearing. She tucked the image of him into the back of her mind to consider later, when she was alone again.

Cecil looked up from the stove where he had something delicious cooking. "Ah, there you are," he said with a smile. Recently divorced, he'd been enthusiastic about having her stay with him while she got her bearings in Gold Valley.

She'd been here for six months and certainly had her bearings, but she hadn't moved out. She and Cecil got along great. He cooked; she did dishes. They both liked Chinese food on Friday nights, and sitting near the back in church on Sundays. And Holland could admit she liked having a friend to come home to at night.

Her labradoodle Lucy came barreling toward the back door, and Holland cooed at her as the dog's whole body wagged back and forth in excitement.

She scrubbed the curly hair on top of Lucy's head. "How are you, you big sheep?" With a big barrel body, her white coloring, and that curly poodle hair, Lucy really did resemble a sheep more than a dog.

Lucy put her paws on Holland's chest, but Holland pushed her down. "Stop it, you moose." She grinned at the dog and pulled the back door closed.

She exhaled heavily as she sat at the bar. "What's that?" she asked, eying the mixture in the pan. It looked like—

"Mushrooms and onions and chicken," he said. "For the calzones."

"Calzones? People actually make those?"

Cecil chuckled and balanced the wooden spoon on the pan's edge to turn his attention to the dough on the counter. He patted it, spooned on the filling, and sealed the pockets expertly. As he slid the tray of egg-washed calzones into a hot oven, Holland reminded herself that he worked in a supermarket all day.

So he was the grocery manager, doing everything from schedules to payroll to ordering, not a chef or anything. But he certainly knew food and how to put it together, for which Holland was grateful. She hadn't had the energy to put more together than bread and peanut butter since her move.

Before that, really. One day she'd admit that everything in her life had changed when she'd started dating Jordan Mickelson.

But that wasn't today, and she leaned into her palms as Cecil started stacking dishes in the sink for her to wash later. "So I met someone today."

He froze, only his eyes moving up to meet hers. "In the home health center? What did we establish about dating patients?"

Holland gave her cousin a smile. "He's not a patient." Because they had established a strict no-dating-patients rule for Holland. "He's a cowboy."

Cecil quirked one eyebrow at her. "How did you meet a cowboy?"

"His father broke his hip. He came down for the family consult." The scent of baking bread filled the house, and Holland took a deep breath, thinking of her mother's cooking.

"So you spoke to him for five seconds," Cecil said, shaking his head. "I know this game."

"He was handsome."

"I thought you were here to work. Get your career started. In fact, I distinctly remember you saying the words 'No dating for me. No sir. Not necessary.'" He settled against the counter opposite her and smirked.

"It's *not* necessary," Holland said, an air of forced nonchalance in her tone. Dating in general wasn't necessary, but dating Elliott Hawthorne…. Well, she'd do everything she could to get assigned to his father, as Elliott would be coming down from the ranch where he worked every evening and she really wanted to know what color of hair hid beneath that delicious cowboy hat.

———

With a chicken and mushroom calzone in her lunchbox, Holland headed into work the next morning earlier than usual. Only ten minutes, but enough to get to the center, stash her lunch, and be in the conference room before anyone else. She was usually one of the last, bustling in with her coffee and an apologetic smile to the director.

But not today. Oh, no. She wanted to be seen first when Kevin walked through the door, maybe even ask about Sean Hawthorne.

With four new cases being assigned today and only two

physical therapists, Holland had a good chance of landing the Hawthorne case.

"Morning, Holland," Kevin said as he entered the room. He carried several folders, and Holland put on her brightest smile and didn't look at what he had in his arms.

"Morning."

"How did things go with the family consult last night?" He sat at the head of the table and pulled a pen out of his breast pocket.

"Great," she said, maybe a little too brightly. "The younger son didn't want to sign the power of attorney."

"That's fine." Kevin didn't even glance up from the paperwork.

"I liked the father," Holland said, though Char had done most of the work with him last night. She was a CNA and had taken the vitals and marked the chart.

"Great." Kevin fanned the folders and tapped one. "Do you want him?"

Holland lifted one shoulder though Kevin hadn't even looked up. "Sure, I'll take him."

He pushed the folder toward her and marked something on his clipboard. "Sounds good. He needs to be seen today."

Holland didn't reach for the folder, though she wanted to grab it and press it to her chest. "I'll schedule a time to get over there."

Two nurses entered the room and Holland fell silent. She'd gotten what she'd wanted, and a giggle threatened to escape her lips. She kept it contained during the meeting, but as soon as she got to her closet of an office, she couldn't help letting it out.

————

"Yes, definitely let your son know what time I'm coming," Holland said later that morning, after calling Sean Hawthorne to set up his physical therapy appointment. "Since I've only been approved to come three times a week, you'll need to do the therapy on your own, and I'd like to train your wife and son so they can help you."

"All right," Sean said. "He works a lot. If he needs to be here, evenings are best."

"I can accommodate your schedule, Mister Hawthorne." Holland wore a smile on her face that translated into her voice.

"Maybe you should call him," Sean said. "I don't know when he'll be done tonight."

Holland's heart started beating to a quick rhythm. "What time is good for you?" she asked. After all, she was getting paid to rehabilitate Sean Hawthorne, not arrange a time to meet his son.

"Anytime that works for Elliott works for us," he said. "Here's his number." He recited the number, and Holland hastened to scratch it on a nearby scrap of paper.

"I'll give him a call," she promised before hanging up.

But she didn't call right away. She wanted to, but she didn't want her excitement to show in her voice. She needed to be professional, aloof, the way she'd been last night.

Business during business hours, she reminded herself.

Still, she waited until she'd consumed her calzone before even attempting to call Elliott. She hadn't called a cute cowboy before, and though she had sworn off dating when she'd left Idaho, her stomach was still a jittery mess.

Properly fed, with carbs in her system, she punched in the necessary numbers. His phone rang and rang, finally going to voicemail. She'd only heard him speak a few words, but when he said, "This is Elliott Hawthorne. I'm probably out of range right now, so leave a message, and I'll call you back," her pulse picked up.

He had a deep, sexy voice that made the hair on the back of her neck stand up. He'd been tall, trim, and tough in the way he'd denied his older brother over the power of attorney.

She cleared her throat just as the beep sounded on his voicemail. "Hello, Elliott," she said in her calmest voice possible. "This is Holland Marsh…."

———

Read LOVE AT FIRST COWBOY today! A career cowboy, a home health nurse, and an instantaneous connection they both try to fight…

Scan the QR code below to get it!

The Redesigned Ranch (Book 1): Jace Lovell, still nursing a wounded heart after being jilted at the altar, has dedicated himself to becoming the best foreman at Horseshoe Home Ranch. When he decides to hire an interior designer to please the ranch owner's wife, he didn't expect to be faced with a familiar face from his past. **Can Belle's patience and faith help Jace find the path to forgiveness and lead them to discover their own slice of happily-ever-after?**

Snowed in with the Cowboy (Book 2): Sterling Maughan, once a renowned snowboarder, is in self-imposed exile at his family cabin after a tragic accident stole his career. Lost and without purpose, solitude is his only companion until an unexpected visitor disrupts his isolation. **Can Norah trust Sterling enough to let him into her life and give their unexpected and forbidden love a chance?**

The Preacher's Daughter (Book 3): Landon Edmunds, a cowboy born and bred, has had his rodeo dreams realized and then dashed by a career-ending injury. Back in his hometown working at Horseshoe Home Ranch, he yearns for a new beginning with a ranch of his own. His sights are set on buying a horse ranch to train rodeo horses, but his plans take a detour when his high school best friend, Megan Palmer, steps back into his life. **Will they choose to follow their hearts, or will they let true love slip through their fingers again?**

Be sure to check out the spinoff series, the Brush Creek Cowboys romances after you read THE PREACHER'S DAUGHTER. Start with BRUSH CREEK COWBOY.

The Cowboy and the Nanny (Book 4): Twelve years ago, Owen Carr traded his roots and his sweetheart in Gold Valley for the bright lights of Nashville, where he found fame as a country music star. But when a tragic accident leaves him single-handedly raising his eight-year-old niece, Marie, he's forced to return home. Overwhelmed and out of his depth, Owen finds a lifeline in a most unexpected place. **As they mend bridges and explore the sparks that still sizzle between them, will they open their hearts to a second chance at love?**

Right Cowboy, Right Time (Book 5): Caleb Chamberlain, a fun-loving cowboy at Horseshoe Home Ranch, has spent the last five years wrestling with the ghosts of his past—a devastating breakup, alcoholism, and a near-fatal accident. Now, he's finally found solace in laughter and the rhythmic simplicity of ranch life. But a chance encounter with a familiar face threatens to upheave his newfound peace. **Can they navigate the shadows of the past to find their happily-ever-after?**

Second Chance Family (Book 6): Ty Barker has been living a carefree existence for the last thirty years. As friends around him found love and started families, Ty filled his time by giving horseback riding lessons and serving on a community service committee. But beneath the jovial surface, he's starting to feel the sting of loneliness. **He knows he wants River Lee in his life—but the question is, can he navigate the delicate steps needed to make her stay with him?**

The Christmas Cowboy Competition (Book 7): Archer Bailey has already had to yield one job to Emersyn "Emery" Enders. So when the opportunity of a cowhand job at Horseshoe Home Ranch presents itself, he keeps it to himself. Emery, whose temporary job is ending but whose responsibilities towards her physically disabled sister aren't, is left in the dark.

As the festive season unfolds, **will Emery and Archer navigate the complexities of the ranch, their close living arrangements, and their personal challenges to discover the love building between them? Or will their rivalry rob them of the greatest Christmas gift of all—true love?**

Love at First Cowboy (Book 8): Elliott Hawthorne, a career cowboy, has just witnessed his best friend and cabinmate forsake bachelorhood for matrimony. He'd be joyous if he weren't so green with envy. When a call about a family accident demands his presence, Elliott finds himself rushing from the ranch to his parents' house to see what's going on with his daddy, where he encounters the most stunning woman he's ever laid eyes on. **But as they encounter the complex dynamics of family responsibilities and personal desires, can their love-at-first-sight grow strong enough withstand the test of time?**

Second Chance Ranch: A Three Rivers Ranch Romance™ (Book 1): After his deployment, injured and discharged Major Squire Ackerman returns to Three Rivers Ranch, wanting to forgive Kelly for ignoring him a decade ago. He'd like to provide the stable life she needs, but with old wounds opening and a ranch on the brink of financial collapse, it will take patience and faith to make their second chance possible.

Third Time's the Charm: A Three Rivers Ranch Romance™ (Book 2): First Lieutenant Peter Marshall has a truckload of debt and no way to provide for a family, but Chelsea helps him see past all the obstacles, all the scars. With so many unknowns, can Pete and Chelsea develop the love, acceptance, and faith needed to find their happily ever after?

Fourth and Long: A Three Rivers Ranch Romance™ (Book 3): Commander Brett Murphy goes to Three Rivers Ranch to find some rest and relaxation with his Army buddies. Having his ex-wife show up with a seven-year-old she claims is his son is anything but the R&R he craves. Kate needs to make amends, and Brett needs to find forgiveness, but are they too late to find their happily ever after?

Fifth Generation Cowboy: A Three Rivers Ranch Romance™ (Book 4): Tom Lovell has watched his friends find their true happiness on Three Rivers Ranch, but everywhere he looks, he only sees friends. Rose Reyes has been bringing her daughter out to the ranch for equine therapy for months, but it doesn't seem to be working. Her challenges with Mari are just as frustrating as ever. Could Tom be exactly what Rose needs? Can he remove his friendship blinders and find love with someone who's been right in front of him all this time?

Sixth Street Love Affair: A Three Rivers Ranch Romance™ (Book 5): After losing his wife a few years back, Garth Ahlstrom thinks he's ready for a second chance at love. But Juliette Thompson has a secret that could destroy their budding relationship. Can they find the strength, patience, and faith to make things work?

The Seventh Sergeant: A Three Rivers Ranch Romance™ (Book 6): Life has finally started to settle down for Sergeant Reese Sanders after his devastating injury overseas. Discharged from the Army and now with a good job at Courage Reins, he's finally found happiness—until a horrific fall puts him right back where he was years ago: Injured and depressed. Carly Watters, Reese's new veteran care coordinator, dislikes small towns almost as much as she loathes cowboys. But she finds herself faced with both when she gets assigned to Reese's case. Do they have the humility and faith to make their relationship more than professional?

Eight Second Ride: A Three Rivers Ranch Romance™ (Book 7): Ethan Greene loves his work at Three Rivers Ranch, but he can't seem to find the right woman to settle down with. When sassy yet vulnerable Brynn Bowman shows up at the ranch to recruit him back to the rodeo circuit, he takes a different approach with the barrel racing champion. His patience and newfound faith pay off when a friendship--and more--starts with Brynn. But she wants out of the rodeo circuit right when Ethan wants to rejoin. Can they find the path God wants them to take and still stay together?

The Ninth Inning: A Three Rivers Ranch Romance™ (Book 8): The Christmas season has never felt like such a burden to boutique owner Andrea Larsen. But with Mama gone and the holidays upon her, Andy finds herself wishing she hadn't been so quick to judge her former boyfriend, cowboy Lawrence Collins. Well, Lawrence hasn't forgotten about Andy either, and he devises a plan to get her out to the ranch so they can reconnect. Do they have the faith and humility to patch things up and start a new relationship?

Ten Days in Town: A Three Rivers Ranch Romance™ (Book 9): Sandy Keller is tired of the dating scene in Three Rivers. Though she owns the pancake house, she's looking for a fresh start, which means an escape from the town where she grew up. When her older brother's best friend, Tad Jorgensen, comes to town for the holidays, it is a balm to his weary soul. A helicopter tour guide who experienced a near-death experience, he's looking to start over too--but in Three Rivers. Can Sandy and Tad navigate their troubles to find the path God wants them to take--and discover true love--in only ten days?

Eleven Year Reunion: A Three Rivers Ranch Romance™ (Book 10): Pastry chef extraordinaire, Grace Lewis has moved to Three Rivers to help Heidi Ackerman open a bakery in Three Rivers. Grace relishes the idea of starting over in a town where no one knows about her failed cupcakery. She doesn't expect to run into her old high school boyfriend, Jonathan Carver. A carpenter working at Three Rivers Ranch, Jon's in town against his will. But with Grace now on the scene, Jon's thinking life in Three Rivers is suddenly looking up. But with her focus on baking and his disdain for small towns, can they make their eleven year reunion stick?

The Twelfth Town: A Three Rivers Ranch Romance™ (Book 11): Newscaster Taryn Tucker has had enough of life on-screen. She's bounced from town to town before arriving in Three Rivers, completely alone and completely anonymous-- just the way she now likes it. She takes a job cleaning at Three Rivers Ranch, hoping for a chance to figure out who she is and where God wants her. When she meets happy-go-lucky cowhand Kenny Stockton, she doesn't expect sparks to fly. Kenny's always been "the best friend" for his female friends, but the pull between him and Taryn can't be denied. Will they have the courage and faith necessary to make their opposite worlds mesh?

Lucky Number Thirteen: A Three Rivers Ranch Romance™ (Book 12): Tanner Wolf, a rodeo champion ten times over, is excited to be riding in Three Rivers for the first time since he left his philandering ways and found religion. Seeing his old friends Ethan and Brynn is therapuetic--until a terrible accident lands him in the hospital. With his rodeo career over, Tanner thinks maybe he'll stay in town--and it's not just because his nurse, Summer Hamblin, is the prettiest woman he's ever met. But Summer's the queen of first dates, and as she looks for a way to make a relationship with the transient rodeo star work Summer's not sure she has the fortitude to go on a second date. Can they find love among the tragedy?

The Curse of February Four-teenth: A Three Rivers Ranch Romance™ (Book 13): Cal Hodgkins, cowboy veterinarian at Bowman's Breeds, isn't planning to meet anyone at the masked dance in small-town Three Rivers. He just wants to get his bachelor friends off his back and sit on the sidelines to drink his punch. But when he sees a woman dressed in gorgeous butterfly wings and cowgirl boots with blue stitching, he's smitten. Too bad she runs away from the dance before he can get her name, leaving only her boot behind...

Fifteen Minutes of Fame: A Three Rivers Ranch Romance™ (Book 14): Navy Richards is thirty-five years of tired—tired of dating the same men, working a demanding job, and getting her heart broken over and over again. Her aunt has always spoken highly of the matchmaker in Three Rivers, Texas, so she takes a six-month sabbatical from her high-stress job as a pediatric nurse, hops on a bus, and meets with the matchmaker. Then she meets Gavin Redd. He's handsome, he's hardworking, and he's a cowboy. But is he an Aquarius too? Navy's not making a move until she knows for sure...

Sixteen Steps to Fall in Love: A Three Rivers Ranch Romance™ (Book 15): A chance encounter at a dog park sheds new light on the tall, talented Boone that Nicole can't ignore. As they get to know each other better and start to dig into each other's past, Nicole is the one who wants to run. This time from her growing admiration and attachment to Boone. From her aging parents. From herself.

But Boone feels the attraction between them too, and he decides he's tired of running and ready to make Three Rivers his permanent home. **Can Boone and Nicole use their faith to overcome their differences and find a happily-ever-after together?**

The Sleigh on Seventeenth Street: A Three Rivers Ranch Romance™ (Book 16): A cowboy with skills as an electrician tries a relationship with a down-on-her luck plumber. Can Dylan and Camila make water and electricity play nicely together this Christmas season? Or will they get shocked as they try to make their relationship work?

The First Lady of Three Rivers Ranch: A Three Rivers Ranch Romance™ (Book 17): Heidi Duffin has been dreaming about opening her own bakery since she was thirteen years old. She scrimped and saved for years to afford baking and pastry school in San Francisco. And now she only has one year left before she's a certified pastry chef.

Frank Ackerman's father has recently retired, and he's taken over the largest cattle ranch in the Texas Panhandle. A horseman through and through, he's also nearing thirty-one and looking for someone to bring love and joy to a homestead that's been dominated by men for a decade. But when he convinces Heidi to come clean the cowboy cabins, she changes all that. But the siren's call of a bakery is still loud in Heidi's ears, even if she's also seeing a future with Frank. Can she rely on her faith in ways she's never had to before or will their relationship end when summer does?

Eighteen Bowties and Counting: A Three Rivers Ranch Romance™ (Book 18): He's her older brother's best friend and completely off-limits. She's got a way with horses...and a heart condition. Can Beau and Charlotte navigate close quarters to find their happily-ever-after?

Last Chance Ranch (Book 1): A cowgirl down on her luck hires a man who's good with horses and under the hood of a car. Can Hudson fine tune Scarlett's heart as they work together? Or will things backfire and make everything worse at Last Chance Ranch?

Last Chance Cowboy (Book 2): A billionaire cowboy without a home meets a woman who secretly makes food videos to pay her debts...Can Carson and Adele do more than fight in the kitchens at Last Chance Ranch?

Last Chance Wedding (Book 3): A female carpenter needs a husband just for a few days... Can Jeri and Sawyer navigate the minefield of a pretend marriage before their feelings become real?

Last Chance Reunion (Book 4): An Army cowboy, the woman he dated years ago, and their last chance at Last Chance Ranch... Can Dave and Sissy put aside hurt feelings and make their second chance romance work?

Last Chance Lake (Book 5): A former dairy farmer and the marketing director on the ranch have to work together to make the cow cuddling program a success. But can Karla let Cache into her life? Or will she keep all her secrets from him - and keep *him* a secret too?

Last Chance Christmas (Book 6): She's tired of having her heart broken by cowboys. He waited too long to ask her out. Can Lance fix things quickly, or will Amber leave Last Chance Ranch before he can tell her how he feels?

Liz Isaacson writes inspirational romance, usually set in Texas, or Wyoming, or anywhere else horses and cowboys exist. She lives in Utah, where she writes full-time, takes her two dogs to the park everyday, and eats a lot of veggies while writing. Find her on her website at feelgoodfiction-books.com